I0671354

Beholden

Inez R. Reilly | Author

Cassandra Allen | Senior Editor

Selma Preston | Continuity Editor

Publisher Sadie Books, 215 East Camden Ave #G-2, Moorestown, NJ 08057 sadie-books.com 856-313-0548

ISBN # 978-0615745039

Cover Art/Interior/Exterior callendesign.com

DEDICATION

I want to express my deepest appreciation to Cassandra Allen for her hard work on the illustration and the cover of this book.

Acknowledgments:

I give all thanks to God, Who is the Author and Finisher of my faith. He gave me the gift, to write. Therefore, He gets all of the credit.

I want to thank my children and grandchildren: Keilah, Joshua, Seraya, Joy, Haliek, Ryan and Sydney. I appreciate their encouragement and their patience, while I took time away from them to complete this project. I want to thank, my very best friend/sister Cherrie Webb, for her prayers and words of inspiration, as I sat for hours working on this book. I am grateful to Cassandra Allen, my media contact @ bullhorngypsy.com, who exhibits blind faith in my abilities, which encourages me to be the best that God intends. Thanks, to my mentors: Pastor Katherine Corbett, Brenda Gonzalez and Brendell Francis – my father and step-mom, Irving Brooks, Sr. and Roberta - my "sisters:" Patricia Ryland-Fisher, Anitrese Sadio, Kandice Corbett, Kenyatta Preston, Mary Berry, Marilyn Coleman, Peggy Whitfield, Monique Tookes, Yvonne Pierre and Mellanese Knockett – my "brothers:" Richard "Poncho" Cabrel, Irving Brooks, Jr., Carlos Brooks, Darryl Brooks, Anthony Brooks, Eddie Corbett, Jr, Frank Corbett and Kirk Knockett - the "older women:" Selma Preston and Kathleen Jones – my nieces and nephews: Nicole, Michael, Lewis, Marianna, Marisol, Nick, Mo, Tony, David, Sylvia, Evelyn, Debra, Levone, LaToya, Nikki, Desiree, Anthony, LeSean, Diondre "Munch", Ashley and Jonathan – Special recognition to those who have supported me, Tia Browne, Joanie Webb, Pamela Hancock, Quentin Haynes, Helen Hinshaw, Tishena Brooks and the countless others who have reassured and succored me through intercession – last, but not least, those of you who purchased this book.

CHAPTER ONE

Mavet's dark eyes scanned the congregation of the Wisdom Outreach Center as they raised their hands in obedience to the worship leader. He chuckled, to himself, at the empty gesture. So many of the churchgoers were like robots during the service. They stood to their feet, clapped and raised their hands, and shouted by direction. Each action was simply a reaction to what was going on up front. Suddenly, a hush came over the sanctuary causing Mavet to avert his attention to the front of the church. A chill swept through the room; however, he could not determine the source of the wind. The tiny hairs on the back of his neck began to rise causing him to lose focus. He felt uneasy and agitated. His eyes narrowed as he moved about the room to pinpoint the origin of the disturbance. He wondered why no one else seemed to be as bothered by this sudden change in the atmosphere as he was. His search took him from row to row until he had maneuvered his way, unhindered, to the front of the church.

Mavet's heart began to race and he quickly turned to see who was standing at the podium; it was Ziva Montgomery, the First Lady of the church. Her beauty was undeniable. It emanated from within her like the flame shining forth from a lantern. Her chestnut brown hair fell gracefully over her shoulders; her crowning glory. Her ivory skin was flawless, requiring very little make-up. This morning she wore an amber colored sundress, with a belt cinched at the waist. Her five-inch heels, matched perfectly, and enhanced her already statuesque aura. She was greeting the members, as was her custom every Sunday that she attended. Her voice was light and very feminine.

"Good morning, saints" she started. "It is such a pleasure to see your smiling faces, on today. It blesses my soul to know that God's love has seen fit to allow us to assemble ourselves together, one more time."

The congregation seemed to love her, but Mavet hated her. She refused to give him his proper respect. She treated him like he didn't matter – like his authority meant nothing to her – like she had greater power – like he couldn't get to her like he had done all the others.

Albeit, he had not even gotten the opportunity to speak to her, face to face, he was certain that she would come around – all he had to do was get her to reveal her weakness, then he would whittle away at it until she begged him to give her the strength to overcome it. In the meantime, Mavet could not argue the fact that she was getting under his skin. That chill was too much to deal with, now. He needed to get away from it because he was beginning to feel ill. His bones seemed to rattle as he shivered uncontrollably. He needed to nuzzle up to a warm and accepting body. He quickly scanned the room and his eyes looked passed Ziva to the doorway just off to her left. He walked to the front, being sure to stay along the wall, so he would not draw attention to himself. He took up his place, directly in front of the tall, dark man standing in the door.

Pastor Zeke Montgomery did not seem to notice Mavet, as he looked out into the congregation. However, he did take note of the empty seats and immediately wondered what he could do to get warm bodies into them. He needed to implement a plan that would help him realize his vision for the Wisdom Outreach Center. He knew God would be pleased as he sought to fulfill his calling. It took some of the wind out of his sails, every time he walked out onto the podium to see there was room for more people. He knew he had a word from the Lord that would benefit so many more than turned out to listen to his sermons. There were hungry and thirsty souls seeking relief from their condition and he was confident that he had the solution to their need. He needed to settle himself down – quiet the cyclical thoughts that plagued him by highlighting those empty chairs. He took a deep breath and Mavet moved closer, and whispered in his ear. The pastor sighed, as he felt his help coming.

Pastor Zeke, as he was accustomed to people addressing him, brushed at his tailor-made navy blue pinstriped suit to insure it was spotless. Ziva always took the lint roller to his suits, every Sunday morning before she greeted Wisdom Outreach parishioners, but he nervously brushed at them just before stepping out onto the podium. He was an opposing figure, standing a full foot taller than the average person. His dark skin, neatly barbered mustache and beard, along with his closely shaved head gave him a distinguished look that caused certain women to pay closer attention to his sermons than they would any other preacher. He thought this would give his gorgeous wife reason to be jealous, yet she remained confident in her place. There was no jealous bone in her, at least none that she let anyone to see. In all of their twenty-five years of marriage, neither of them had strayed or even caused the other any worry. Their love was strong and solid, built on the foundation of Christ. He smiled as he listened to Ziva encourage and exhort the congregation. The people loved her, too – and for that, he was most grateful. Their eyes met, she smiled and gave him an imperceptible nod giving him the okay to join her at the podium.

"...and here he is, our beloved Pastor Zeke. Please stand to your feet and show him some love." Ziva Montgomery held out her hand waiting for Pastor Zeke to take it into his own. He approached her and kissed her lovingly on the forehead.

Mavet took up the position, vacated by Pastor Zeke, as he went to stand next to his wife, Ziva. He couldn't stand to be around her – she was so discourteous. He moved further away from the couple and away from the chill. He watched the two of them banter back and forth while engaging the congregation. He looked out amongst the people and his eyes locked with one parishioner, in particular. He felt a welcoming beckon from her, so he eased down the stairs and headed in her direction. She looked so forlorn and in need of his attention. He sensed an emptiness on the inside of her that created a hunger that seemed insatiable. He knew what she needed the moment he positioned himself next to her, on the pew. He asked her a question, and she was quick to share her deepest secrets. He consoled her with promises – promises that she quickly accepted. He encouraged her to rest her head on his shoulder, as they watched the pastor and his wife appear so syncopated and in-step. He recognized her longing and assured her that there was no reason to feel that way.

Maren Dane, the church administrator, sat watching Pastor Zeke and First Lady Ziva wondering why she could not have that in her marriage. She fidgeted in her seat. She smoothed her skirt down. She fussed with her hair. She admired the First Lady and felt she paled in comparison. Although Lady Ziva was ten years her senior, she didn't look a day over thirty-five. Maren, on the other hand, with her slightly out of shape body and crow's feet around her eyes, appeared to be far older than her forty years. She wore girdles and other body shapers, in an attempt to hide her love of food – but, she was unsuccessful. Her *secrets* were always visible. She hated standing beside Lady Ziva because she felt so uncomfortable. It was nothing that the First Lady said or did to make her so insecure. In fact, she was nothing short of accepting and loving. Yet, Maren could not shake the discomfort. She began to nit-pick her own appearance. She second-guessed her clothing choice and her make-up, whenever Lady Ziva stopped by the pastor's office.

Maren reached out her hand to touch her husband's hand. Adley was engrossed in the exchange happening at the front of the church. He barely felt her hand resting on top of his. She imagined he was wishing that she could be more like the First Lady. She quickly removed her hand and placed them on her lap. Mavet watched as Maren chided herself. *This is too easy*, he thought to himself. He patted her hand, gently – and more secrets unfolded. His words kept her distracted, so she could not focus on the sermon. The louder Pastor Zeke spoke, the closer Mavet drew to Maren. Her eyes welled up with tears as her shortcomings became more evident. Her eyes darted from woman to woman and couple to couple. They were the lucky ones. They had shapely bodies.

They had smooth skin. They had attentive husbands. They had children. They had stylish clothing. The thoughts were on repeat; and no matter how much she tried to fill her mind with other things, they refused to stop. She found herself becoming more and more agitated – then her agitation turned to anger.

Mavet sat back and watched her walls crumble before his very eyes. Maren Dane would not be a problem, at all. She flung the door wide open at the slightest bit of consideration. He wanted to move about the church, but she demanded his full attention. He gave her what she wanted, although his focus was divided. Ziva Montgomery was troubling him. Her calm and peaceful demeanor annoyed him and caused him great angst. He became dark and brooding while he watched her sitting in her assigned seat on the pulpit. She glowed as her husband spoke passionately to the dulled crowd. There were only a scant few fully engaged, and following along with bibles and notes. More parishioners were checking their cell phones, posting updates to Facebook, sending text messages and reading their timelines on twitter. He noticed there were some people holding their own conversations while the pastor was delivering his message. He shook his head. He didn't understand what compelled them to come to church. Sunday after Sunday they filed into the pews, got comfortable and bided their time until the benediction. *What a waste of time!* He scoffed.

Pastor Zeke was finishing his sermon. He was bringing his point home. He wanted the congregation to be fully cognizant of the love of God and that it is unconditional. There is no sin that will cause His love to falter – it is unfailing. His love should not be compared with the love that is experienced between humans.

"We keep records of the wrong done to us. We are grudge holders. Even though, God tells us that this is not how love is expressed, we choose our way over all else. We refuse to put another's feelings above our own. We refuse to *not* be offended. We refuse to set aside petty differences for the sake of unity. This is not God's love. John 3:16 is a perfect example of His love ...'For God so loved the world that He gave...'" Pastor Zeke asserted.

Lady Ziva stood to her feet. Her face shone radiantly as she raised her hands and closed her eyes. She allowed herself to experience God's love on a daily basis. His love kept her sane and at peace with her life. She knew there was nothing that she could do that would demand that she forfeit the love of God. She could come to Him, during prayer, without fear because He would never turn her away. His love believes all things – His loves believes that she wants to do the right thing and please Him, above all else. His love does not force her to comply; it simply compels her to want what He wants. His love refuses to twist her arm, demanding that she do His will. His Holy Spirit whispers to her spirit and she responds with an open heart and a willing mind. If it were not for the love of God, she would not be able to handle her calling as a wife of a pastor or the mother of a pastor's kids. The days could be draining with the demands of her time, her patience, her long-suffering, her compassion and her love. God opened up her heart – and continues to do so – allowing her to be up for the challenges that face her, on a daily basis. As difficult as it could be, God gave her the strength and the wherewithal to embrace her life with joy.

Maren's attention was drawn to the pulpit where Lady Ziva was worshiping God. She noticed how serene her face appeared with her hands outstretched. She glanced over at

Adley, her husband, and noticed that he was looking in the same direction. He raised his hands and offered his praise, quietly, to God for His love. She wanted him to look at her the same way he was ogling the First Lady. She leaned closer to him and called his name, sharply, under her breath. That snapped him out of his reverie and he turned toward his wife. His face showed his displeasure at her rude interruption, but she was undeterred. She did not want him fantasizing about the First Lady while she stood right next to him. She asked him for their tithes, so she could place it in the envelope and fill out their information. He reached into his suit pants to pull out his wallet and counted out the money. He handed the bills to her, about to turn his attention back to the pulpit, but Maren asked for a pen. He pulled a pen out of the inside pocket of his suit jacket and handed it to his wife. He paused waiting to see if there would be any other requests...there were none.

Pastor Zeke finished his sermon and moved into the offering portion of the service. He encouraged the congregation to give joyfully. God loves a cheerful giver; he reminded them. Offering time allows God's children to sow into His kingdom – it gives the church seed to sow into the community and the other mission projects they have going on. Every person has an opportunity to experience the joy of giving, no matter the size of the offering. There should be no hindrances to their giving, as this was between the congregant and God. He invited his wife up to the podium to stand with him in their giving. She stood beside him and rubbed his back. She whispered something to him and they smiled, in unison. He took her hand into his and kissed it before turning back to the congregation. He gave the ushers the word and they began to pass the offering baskets to the first person on each row. They scouted out the occasional person who needed an envelope or requested a pen. Once completed, they brought the baskets to the front of the church and poured the contents into a larger basket.

Pastor Zeke raised his one free hand, as did First Lady Ziva, and he began to pray. "Father, we bring to You the first fruits of our labor and an offering. We understand that You do not need our money; it is just an opportunity for us to participate in expanding Your kingdom, here on earth. We appreciate this chance to be a part of what You are doing. We are filled with joy knowing that we can be Your hands and bless those who are seeking relief. You said, give and it shall be given unto you – good measure, pressed down and running over shall men give unto your bosom. We gladly take up the charge to be the man *and woman* used to give back to those who are trusting You to supply their needs. We give You the glory and the honor for giving us the seed to sow into Your kingdom. We trust You to take care of us, as we seek to take care of Your people. We bless You and give You the praise. In Jesus name, we pray – Amen and thank God."

The ushers took the basket out of the sanctuary and into the finance office, as was the custom and Pastor Zeke called for those who wanted to accept God's love gift, embodied in Jesus Christ.

"There is no greater love than for one to lay down his life for his brother. Christ embraced the cross and all that it entailed, so we could be reconciled to the Father. God sent His Son into the world, not to condemn the world, but to save us from the path of destruction that we were headed down. His love wants us filled with joy – a state of acceptance of His love no matter our circumstances. His love wants us filled with peace – a heart condition that remains calm in the midst of tests and trials. Will you come?" Pastor Zeke opened his arms to accept those who walked down the aisle, all the while longing for the time when more people would come to join the church. He wanted the seats filled.

Mavet smiled, as he stood next to Pastor Zeke speaking into his ear.

CHAPTER TWO

The atmosphere, in the car, belied the message they just heard preached by Pastor Zeke. The tension and anxiety was thick and palpable. Katriel removed her iPod from her purse and put the ear buds into her ears. She turned the volume up just enough to drown out her father's words. She hated when he was like this, especially after church service. She had been feeling a bit hopeful listening to the sermon on love and its unconditional nature. She wanted to believe that there was such a thing out there in the world, because she sure as hell did not recognize it in her own home. She could not understand what her father had to be angry about, this morning. Breakfast was prepared and still hot when he made it to the table, prior to them leaving for church. Her mother had seemed to be in a good mood despite the fact that she had an emergency surgery to perform in the wee hours of the morning. She could not have had more than two hours of sleep before taking up her place in the kitchen to prepare the morning meal. Katriel felt good about the day...but her father quickly snatched the joy right out of the air.

"I don't understand why they could not have called another surgeon in to do the procedure. You mean to tell me that you are the only pediatric cardiologist at Mercy Medical Center, Nora?" The venom in Gavin's voice was evident.

"Like I told you, Gavin, the little girl is my patient. Of course, they would not call another surgeon in to take care of her. It is my responsibility," Nora's words were soft.

"You seem to have quite a list of patients, Nora. What kind of doctor can you be, if all of the children you care for need so much attention? Can't you do anything right?"

Nora remained silent. She hated when Gavin was like this. His words were intentionally hurtful and mean. She spoke a silent prayer asking God to eradicate the effects of his words. She knew she was a good doctor and surgeon. She knew that he was just acting this way because the call came in after they had gone to bed and it disturbed his rest. She knew he could not mean what he was saying …he was just angry. She turned her head to look out of the passenger side window. They had been sitting at a light and she realized the people in the car next to them could hear Gavin. The woman looked pitiably in her direction, and then sped off once the light turned green.

"I know you hear me talking to you, Nora. You better give me an answer. What the hell did you do to that little girl that required her to need emergency surgery in the middle of the night? You're a quack! I don't understand how you keep your job," he spat the words, like a bitter gall, in her direction.

"Gavin, she has a grave condition called aortic valve insufficiency…" Nora began.

"Don't come at me with those grand diagnoses, Nora. It does not concern me what she has, just that you are the one caring for her and she is not getting any better."

Nora sighed and gave up the illusion that she could convince her husband. It had been a long while, if ever, since she could say anything that would sway him one way or the other. She returned her attention to the passing landscape. She resisted the urge to cry. It would only make things worse. She felt most sad that Katriel, their sixteen-year-old daughter, had to be a witness to her father's tirades. She did not want her child to grow up in an environment as she did. Her mother and father were constantly at war with each other, when she was younger. Both gave to fits of rage and she could not wait until she could get out from under their roof. There was not a day that went by that did not end with her parents being at each other's throat. One or the other had a bad day at work, which spawned a torrential and heated debate between the two of them. Her mother slammed pots and pans while her father slammed doors and she would sit quietly in her room waiting for one of them to yell out her name for some reason or other.

An ominous silence filled the rest of the ride home. Gavin was seething, as he made his way down the street to their home. He just wanted some peace, in his life. His job, as chief of police, was stressful enough. He had a bunch of idiots working under him and he had an incompetent wife with a grandiose profession. It embarrassed him that she could not do her job well enough. He was sure their friends and neighbors knew she was called to the hospital at all hours of the night. He was also certain that they knew it was because she did not do her job right the first time, which was the cause of so many trips to Mercy. For all he knew, she did this on purpose just so she did not have to be at home taking care of her responsibilities. He should not have to be disturbed by the incessant buzzing of her beeper or her hushed tones on the phone when speaking to the after-hours receptionist. He needed his sleep if he was to perform his duties at work and her job was keeping him from getting it. His lack of sleep made him irritable and she knew it.

He turned into the Eagle Ridge subdivision and made his way to their home on Long Creek Lane. He pressed the remote to have the garage door open before turning into the driveway. He eased his car into the empty space, next to Nora's, put the car in 'park' and turned it off. After pulling the key out of the ignition, he turned to his wife and sighed. She knew not to get out of the car until he was ready. He just looked at her, in disgust. He remembered when things were much simpler. They dated throughout college. He was a criminal justice major and she was working toward her doctorate. She was the older woman that caught his attention on campus. She walked with an air of confidence that intrigued him. He told his frat brothers that he was going to have her and they laughed him to shame. He proved them wrong and he was the one laughing when it was all said and done. He had persuaded her to allow him to take her to dinner, one autumn evening. He knew he was charming and had a way to make any woman feel good about herself. Even if he did not believe what he was saying, he could convince them to believe it. He really did a number on Nora.

She quickly turned the tables on him and got herself pregnant. He should have known she was the type that wanted to trap a good man, like himself. He did the honorable thing and married her to keep her quiet. She nagged him about being an unwed mother, and how that would hurt her parents. She should have thought about that before she engaged in unprotected sex, with him. He never understood why she wasn't on birth control, in the first place. She had the unmitigated gall to expect him to wear a condom. He insisted that he would not get any pleasure out of the deal, wearing one of those, and he refused every time. She was so selfish. None of the other girls complained about it, he did not know why she was making such a big deal. The only thing he could think of was that she was only concerned about her own orgasm. She knew he came faster without one, he told her so. It was no surprise to him when she blamed him for her unplanned pregnancy, but he quickly let her know who was to blame. It was her fault, not his.

When Katriel was born, Nora had finished her finals and was preparing for residency. There was no way she could keep those hours and care for a newborn, so her parents suggested that they move in with them and they would take on the responsibility of caring for the baby. Gavin was furious at the notion and even angrier when Nora agreed. He thought she should have given up her idea of becoming a doctor once they had gotten married and Katriel appeared. He was finishing graduate school and accepted into the police academy, which was used as part of her argument why moving in with her parents was a good idea. It would allow them to pursue their dreams with assurance that Katriel well taken care of by people who loved her. When he suggested that Nora stay home with the baby, she flat out refused. She asserted that her having a baby did not warrant such a drastic decision. She had been working toward becoming a doctor since she began high school and she was too close to give that up. He told her that she should have thought about that before getting herself knocked up. She gave him an incredulous look and walked out of the room. She learned that day not to walk away from him.

Despite his objections, Nora did not quit her job and they moved in with her parents so her parents could care for the baby. He had to admit, if only to himself, that this arrangement worked out for the best. He did not have to concern himself with a crying baby and Nora's residency hours left him plenty of time to do what he wanted. He spent many nights out drinking with his fellow academy mates and they spent most of those nights carousing with young, impressionable girls. Just because Nora wanted to be bound by the sanctity of marriage and monogamy, it did not mean that was the life for him. He was still young and in his prime; one woman was not enough for him, he needed more. And, more is what he had gotten. He did not know how many women he let ride him in the back of his car, and he didn't care. Also, not one time did they request he wear a condom, as his wife had done back in college. Besides, Nora was too busy with rounds that she did not have the time to satisfy him, so what was a man to do?

He smiled, to himself, at the memory. He looked back on his academy days, often. He was top of his class and his instructors advised he would go far. He aspired to be commissioner, someday, but he first had to endure the process. He hated having to walk the beat early in his career. He had hoped that rite of passage would have been extinct before he would have to do it. He hated the elderly women looking down at him and advising that he should be doing more to keep their streets safe. He took his anger out on the street thugs who thought they were tough. He would usher them into the nearest alley and give them a beat down with his nightstick. It was rare that he made an arrest, because he didn't want them complaining to higher ups, so he warned them and sent them on their way. He shook down the local drug dealer, confiscating his goods and distributing them amongst his comrades. He became very familiar with the local prostitutes, as well. There was never a shortage of eager women willing to do anything to not be taken down and booked at the precinct.

Katriel ended his reverie. "Can we get out of the car, now?"

"Get out!" He barked.

Once inside, Katriel proceeded up the stairs to her bedroom and closed the door. She did not want to be bothered with the foolishness that had become her parents. She could not wait until she finished high school and could leave the confines of this house. She worked hard not to hate her father and even harder to not think her mother weak. She did not understand why she tolerated her father's constant railing. Her mother was a successful surgeon. She made plenty of money and could easily survive without her father's income. Sure, he made a decent living, but he was not the breadwinner of the family. She knew that had to grate on him. The fact that a woman made more money than him had to be degrading. He walked around their house as if he was the king of the castle and her mother allowed it. Her mother never threw it up in her father's face that her salary trumped his. She could have, but never did. Katriel did not think she would have let an opportunity go by without reminding him that he was not needed to sustain this household. For this reason, she was going to make sure that she and her husband were on equal terms, financially. No one would be able to lord anything over the other one. Moreover, even though her father did not earn respect, her mother always gave it to him anyway.

Katriel threw herself onto her bed and looked out of the window. She heard her mother's footsteps coming up their stairway and hoped she was not heading to her room. She hated it when she wanted to excuse and apologize for her father's behavior. It was not for her to do. He should be the one making amends and smoothing things over. She remembered the pastor talking about how the husband was supposed to love the wife as Christ loved the church. She did not believe her father loved her mother. He tolerated her and that infuriated Katriel. How dare he think he deserved the love and respect her mother wasted on him. He did nothing to earn it. He was constantly degrading her and belittling her contribution to the staff at Mercy. He was not the doting husband of an acclaimed pediatric cardiologist. Instead, he was the tyrant of 7 Long Creek Lane. He patrolled the rooms of this house, as if he patrolled the streets back in the day. He ranted and raved. He flailed and flung. He stormed and raged. He was pathetic. Her mother had to know it, yet she never showed it. She tolerated his tantrums and appeased the spoiled beast.

She breathed a sigh of relief when she heard the door of her parents' bedroom close. Her mother was probably crying or praying. Katriel was sure that was the only thing that kept her feet planted in this marriage – prayer. She wondered how much relief she could really be getting from it, when it seemed like there was no change. Did God even hear her? Her father appeared to be getting worse by the day. There were times when she hoped he would be killed on the job. She felt bad for thinking such a terrible thing about her father, but she could not help it. He didn't deserve to be breathing the same air as those who sought to make life better for those around them. He swore to uphold justice in the world, yet he was the source of all the injustice that happened within these four walls. Why couldn't someone just put a bullet in his head? She knew he had to have a multitude (or gaggle, as her mom would say) of enemies out there who wished for his demise. She and her mom would be much better off if he was not in the picture.

Gavin closed the door to his study and walked over to the bar. He poured himself a glass of Angel's Envy bourbon and sat down in his leather recliner. He turned to look out onto expansive lawn in the back of his house. The patio was just off to the left and he caught sight of the fire pit and chairs surrounding it. He walked out into the yard, through the glass doors, and headed toward the seats. He thought of starting a fire and decided against it – it was too hot. He eased himself onto one of the lounge chairs and put his feet up. He sensed a presence behind him and turned to see Mavet standing close by.

"She doesn't get it, does she Gavin?" Mavet asked, as he sat in nearby chair.

"No," Gavin sipped his drink.

"I understand."

"I know you do. You seem to be the only one who does," he downed the rest of the bourbon, closed his eyes and sighed.

Mavet drew closer. "Talk to me, Gavin."

He allowed his anger to spill out of him, in a rush. He opened up, exposing all of his inner turmoil and rage. He enjoyed the license Mavet gave him and he took the opportunity to bare his soul.

CHAPTER THREE

She became more and more displeased as she listened to the wedding planner drone on about the expense of the wedding. Granted, at the onset Analise Mitchell set a twenty-five thousand dollar budget for the big day, and now she was grossly over-budget – but, it was not Mitrice Reynolds' problem. She was hired to do a job and managing her money was not it. This was her wedding and she would have everything she wanted no matter what it cost. She was only getting married once in her life and it was going to be perfect. She would have the one hundred Ecuadorian roses, even if it cost over fifteen hundred dollars to have them. Mitrice was overstepping her boundaries by advising that she went with some American roses, to bring the cost down. She stepped even further over the line asking her to reconsider the traveling top shelf bartender, as that three-thousand five-hundred dollar expense could be drastically reduced by eliminating the alcohol altogether.

"Mitrice, this is my wedding – not yours."

"I know this, Analise. However, you hired me to plan this wedding with a budget in mind."

"Forget the budget! Just do what I tell you to do and shut up about everything, else." Analise walked across the sitting room and positioned herself in front of the desk.

Mitrice took a deep breath and uttered a quick prayer. "Fine, Analise."

"Good. Now, let's get back to the plans. We don't have long; the wedding is in two weeks." Analise smiled and made her way back to the sofa to sit next to Mitrice.

"The venue is established. We will have the decorators in Turner Hall on Thursday, the nineteenth, to set up for the wedding and the reception. The caterer is prepared for the rehearsal dinner on Friday, the twentieth," Mitrice turned the pages of her planner as she spoke.

Analise smiled as she listened to Mitrice go on about the wedding. As her mind raced with the idea that she could have more, Ghrelin walked through the patio door and sat beside her on the sofa. She sighed at his closeness and the smile grew on her lips. *Yes*, she thought, *I can have more*. Ghrelin agreed with her. He gave her ideas and ways she could make it happen. Any inclination towards a new budget was melting away, as she entertained musings of just how grand her big day could be.

"I want theatrical lighting," Analise burst out.

"Excuse me?" Mitrice asked.

"I want theatrical lighting as I come down the aisle. I want this moment to be surreal and dramatic. My entrance should be memorable and magical."

Mitrice shook her head, imperceptibly. "Turner Hall can accommodate that, I am sure."

Analise clapped her hands, together, and her eyes shone in delight. Ghrelin smiled. He was happy, as long as she was happy. He wanted her to want more. It gave him great pleasure to be a witness to her seemingly insatiable appetites. In fact, he was the one who coaxed her on. The two of them have been buddies since she was a little girl. Her parents catered to her every whim. The more she wanted, the more they gave her. The Mitchells withheld nothing from their little girl. She was their only child and she deserved the best things, in life.

Ghrelin introduced himself to Analise on her first day of school. Her mother dressed her in the finest clothes. She had the latest new thing in snacks, in her lunchbox. She had the prettiest pencils in her flowery pencil case. Ghrelin said hello to her as she looked at Patricia's pink Barbie doll case. He saw the countenance on her face changed, as she became dissatisfied with what her parents had brought her. He agreed that she should be able to have two pencil cases; and looked around as she reached over to grab Patricia's case, while the other children were lining up to go out for recess.

"I'm just going to look at it," she told Ghrelin.

"I know, Analise. It is okay," he assured her.

She slipped the pencil case into her backpack before skipping off to the playground. Ghrelin followed behind her as she headed toward the swings. She swung her legs, to get herself moving and he stood behind her to push her. They talked and giggled with each other, as the other children raced around the yard.

Once they returned inside and Patricia could not find her Barbie pencil case, Ghrelin looked at Analise and smiled. She was scared that

Ghrelin would tell everyone that she had the pencil box. Instead, he put his finger to his mouth. Ms. Harris, the teacher, asked everyone if they had seen it. No one confessed, not even when Patricia cried. Harold volunteered to help her look for it when the teacher thought she might have taken it out on the playground. However, when the teacher's assistant, Ms. Cora, walked them out the bigger kids were out there playing tag. They were racing back and forth so fast that Patricia was afraid they would hurt her. She told Ms. Cora that it did not matter, anymore. She would ask her mother and father for another one.

"Are you sure, sweetie?" Ms. Cora asked as she kneeled down beside her.

"Yes, it's ok," Patricia whimpered.

Ms. Cora took Patricia's hand, then Harold's, and headed back to the classroom. As they walked back in, Analise did not know what she was feeling. She knew she was afraid because she thought she could get into trouble for taking the pencil case. She knew she was not sorry about it, because she wanted it and there was no reason she shouldn't have it. However, there was something else going on in her tummy. Something she had not felt before today.

Ghrelin was smiling at her. He would keep her secret, he whispered. When he said that, the feeling in her tummy went away. She was happy that he was able to make her feel better. From that moment on, they were inseparable. They played together, at school. He came over and played at her house. Her parents let him come with them on vacation. They shared many secrets and he never asked her for anything. He always encouraged her to strive for more. He stood by her throughout school, then on to college. He was her confidante and very best friend.

"Analise, have you heard anything I have been saying?" Mitrice asked.

"Whaa... What?"

"I am going to need a check for the additional funds needed to take care of the new additions you have requested."

"Of course, you are. Hold on, let me go get my checkbook," Analise scurried off to retrieve her purse out of her bedroom.

While Analise was out of the room, Ghrelin looked at Mitrice. He wondered why they had never had a personal conversation. She sat quietly on the sofa, looking through her planner and making notes. He could not read her. He did not talk to her because she seemed aloof and standoffish. On the many occasions they have had to converse, they never hit it off. She was a beautiful woman, with a good head on her shoulders. She was intelligent and confident in her abilities. He wondered why she was planning everyone's wedding, except her own. She was a successful young woman, with her own business. Yet, there were no suitors - at least, none that he ever heard her speak about. Mitrice kept her thoughts to herself. He knew she grew pensive, from time to time, but she never voiced her musings around him or with Analise.

Ghrelin watched Mitrice out of the corner of his eye. He was searching for a conversation starting point, but there seemed to be none. He decided to take a wild guess and see if she had any secret aspirations that she wanted fed. He asked about her childhood. He asked about her college life. He asked about her relationships. They had nothing in common. At every turn, he grew quiet. He decided he would go into the bedroom to see what was keeping Analise. He got up from the sofa and walked toward the back of the house.

He could hear her talking to someone on the phone.

"...yes, sweetie. We are getting the final touches completed on the wedding. I am just writing the check for the last minute expenses," she was walking back and forth by the bedroom window.

Ghrelin stood outside the door. He never interrupted her when Miles was around. He knew people would think that once she became engaged that their relationship would change. In fact, it was quite the opposite. They were closer than ever. He knew his position and he did not overstep his place. He and Analise had been around one another long enough for him to know his role in her life. It was important for the two of them to maintain other relationships. She had Miles and he had … well, he had whomever he chose. The field was ripe with willing companions looking for intimacy on many levels. Some invited him home for a brief, but in-depth chat. While others, met him only in public and did not want to be alone with him. They needed someone to boost their confidence - someone to give permission to proceed when they grew cautious.

"The pastor wants to meet with us, tomorrow evening, for our final counseling session. He is certain we are as prepared as we can be for our marriage," she advised. She twirled her hair as she talked with her fiancé.

Ghrelin smiled. She became such a "girl" when she talked with Miles. Her voice grew light just as it had done when she talked to her father. He knew it was her way of convincing them of her dependence on them. To some degree, she did need them. She had needs and why should she be the one to foot the bill for them? When she used her soft voice with her father, he would give her anything she asked for, no matter the cost. She has been working on Miles for quite some time. He was not exactly her father, but she was not beyond calling him 'daddy' if that was going to accomplish her goal; a long time ago, she realized the best way to broach the subject of getting what she wanted with Miles. She was laying this foundation, right now. She wanted Miles to foot the bill for her overindulgence in the wedding plans. Sure, she would write the check, now. Nevertheless, later tonight she would ensure that she would get it all back.

"I am looking forward to seeing you, later, handsome," she purred into the phone. "I miss your hands on my skin."

The bait was being set. Ghrelin knew her tricks. He had taught her most of them. Over the years, she had asked for his opinion on such matters. He was eager to divulge any secrets he knew to help her obtain the objects of her desire. During college, they were a force to be reckoned with. There was no one who could resist it when they worked together and she had her heart or mind set on getting something.

Analise returned the phone to the receiver, grabbed her checkbook and walked out into the hall. She was not startled to see Ghrelin when she stepped outside of her bedroom door. They smiled at one another and walked back down the hall to the living room. They approached the sofa, together, smiling as if they had just shared a secret.

"I apologize for taking so long. I was on the phone with Miles, alerting him of the latest update on the wedding plans," she sat down next to Mitrice.

"It is quite alright. I had a couple of things to jot down and a phone call to make, as well," Mitrice answered, as she closed her planner.

Analise retrieved a pen off the coffee table and made out the check to Mitrice Reynolds. She ripped it out and handed it to the event planner.

"Thank you, Mitrice," Analise stated as she rose and headed toward the front door.

Ghrelin just smiled at the snub. Analise never wasted time with those she thought was beneath her. Anyone in a service job, such as Mitrice, was there to do her bidding and nothing more. He often shook his head at the irony of her prejudice. To some, a biology teacher was a service job, no matter it was for honors students. However, Analise found a way to over-inflate her career choice. She was molding the minds of the future and preparing them to take their place in society. Yes, it was an honorable profession, yet she was just a part of the working class as those she chose to rebuff.

Mitrice took no offense at the apparent and rude dismissal. She could not take Analise seriously. She did not entertain her ignorant gestures of grandeur. She simply placed the check into her briefcase, along with her planner, grabbed her purse and took her leave. She had too much to do to allow this to deter her. She walked down the front porch and up the driveway to her car. She reached into her suit jacket pocket, pulled out her keys and pressed the remote entry button to unlock the doors. She placed her briefcase on the backseat, closed the door and stepped inside. The stillness of the car's cabin was a relief. There was so much going on, in the atmosphere of Analise's home. She could feel her spirit's uneasiness each time she stepped foot across the threshold; and she always welcomed the fresh air when she left. She leaned her head back against the leather headrest and quietly prayed. This had become her custom after her departure from her clients. She would not allow the atmosphere from one person to hitchhike with her to another appointment.

She prayed until her spirit was at rest and she felt the tension leave her body. She put the key into the ignition, looked into the rearview mirror and slowly backed out of the driveway, turning left to head up Heatherdowns Lane toward North Brodrecht Road. She needed a change of scenery. She wanted to ride through the countryside and knew just the place that could allow that to happen - the Shenandoah Riding Center. She had a favorite horse, which the owners always made available for her, if she alerted them of her intentions. She pushed the button on her dash and called out "Shenandoah Riding Center" to dial the number by voice command. She listened to the ring, hoping no one had taken the horse out this afternoon.

"Shenandoah Riding Center, Connie speaking," the woman answered professionally.

"Hello Connie, this is Mitrice Reynolds. I am heading your way and hoping that Buttercup is available for a ride, this afternoon."

"Yes, she is available, Ms. Reynolds. When can I expect you?" Connie inquired.

"I am in the neighborhood, just leaving a client's home. I can be there in less than five minutes. I hope this isn't too short of notice," Mitrice crossed her fingers.

"No, not at all, Ms. Reynolds. I will have the stable-hand prepare her for your arrival."

Mitrice thanked Connie and they ended the call. When she arrived at the corner of Heatherdowns Lane and North Brodrecht Road, she made a right and headed toward the center.

CHAPTER FOUR

The morning after has such great benefits. Galia Fitzhugh smiled at her reflection, in the bathroom mirror. Her skin glowed. Her hair shone. Her demeanor was most serene. Phineas had a way of making her feel sensual and feminine, even after twenty-five years of marriage. He took special care to ensure her complete satisfaction (sometimes two and three times). He did not seem to mind that things were not quite as perky as they once had been. In fact, it appeared to Galia that he was even more enamored with her more mature body than he had been with her youthful one. If that was not the case, she sure did feel that way – and that is what counted, she encouraged herself. She wondered if the townspeople of Galena knew the things their mayor did behind closed doors; they would blush. As it were, Galia was blushing. She touched her face and felt its warmth as the blood rushed to her cheeks. *After all this time, the thought of this man still makes me blush*, she thought to herself.

Galia remembered her first encounter with Phineas Fitzhugh. He was walking across the campus of the University of Wisconsin. He was a transfer student from Pennsylvania and she was a freshman. He was of average height with bright red hair and green eyes. He looked like his hair was on fire as the sun shone through his curly locks. She had been sitting under a tree reading a book and per chance looked up, just as he was approaching. She was taken aback by his presence. Even though he was not tall, he commanded her attention. He had an air of confidence exuding through his pores that she had not witnessed before...and those eyes! She found herself staring into them, mesmerized. She was so captivated that she had not noticed his hand outstretched, as he introduced himself.

"Excuse me?" Galia stammered.

"Hello. My name is Phineas...Phineas Fitzhugh," he repeated.

His hand was still outstretched. Galia took his hand, this time, and he helped her up from the ground. His broad shoulders silhouetted her petite frame. She looked up into his face and met with a warm smile.

"And who, if I may ask, do I have the pleasure of standing before?" Phineas asked.

"Oh, my name is Galia Chandler," she answered.

"I am pleased to make your acquaintance, Galia."

"Likewise."

"Well, I am new to the campus and to the area. I am a transfer student from Pennsylvania and I need some assistance," he continued.

"How may I help you?" Galia asked. She felt her hand getting warm and she realized that Phineas had not let it go. She did not move it.

"I am looking for North Hall. Can you help me?"

Galia felt herself growing flush at the closeness of his body and the warmth of her hand in his. She had never experienced this before. She berated herself for being swayed so easily. She did not want to come across like other girls, her age, which have just left the confines of their parents' house. She had heard stories of young girls falling for college boys and having to return home, pregnant and ashamed.

She was not going to humiliate her family by becoming one of them. She removed her hand and stepped back.

"I can show you better than I can tell you," she answered. She reached down to retrieve her book and blanket, but was not quite as fast as Phineas. He picked up her items and handed them to her before she could get them herself.

"Lead the way, madam."

The fateful day Galia coined 'the day her life began.' She did not have to fear becoming one of the town's embarrassments, because Phineas Fitzhugh was a complete gentleman. He proved to be very different from the other boys from the east coast. Her friends told her that he was after one thing and they knew she would give in. Most of them were deflowered by college boys and were spending nights in the dorms with some of the boys. Yet, none of them was coming to pick them up or take them out. They would call on the dorm phone and the girls would go out to meet them. Galia was not one of those girls.

"Don't snub your nose up at me," Delores Hammond told her once, as she was heading out after curfew. "You wait, Phineas will be calling you and you will be doing the same thing."

Galia was so grateful that Phineas never called and asked her to break curfew to come entertain him with nighttime activities. Their encounters were in the daylight and magical. He wooed her with his gallantry and she was smitten. They held hands, often. They took walks around the campus and shared lunch almost daily. When she was not feeling well, he came to the dorm's common area with soup and sandwiches. He would bring a blanket and a book. After they ate, he would wrap her in the blanket, sit next to her on the sofa and read to her, from Shakespeare. Even though he was a Political Science major, Phineas was in love with literature. In fact, he read to her quite often under the tree where they met.

It was on one of those occasions that Galia grew pensive. She had begun to fear that Phineas would grow weary of their casual acquaintance. She wondered if he would soon ask her to have sex with him because the other boys were always asking the girls in her dorm. She was even a bit more concerned that she would feel obligated to give in. She enjoyed his company, so much, and did not want to jeopardize it by being a prude. He must have sensed her turmoil.

"What's going on in that pretty little head of yours?" He asked, as he turned to look her in the eyes.

"Well," she started. "I was wondering when you were going to ask me to …" she could not bring herself to say it. She put her head down and sighed.

"Ask you what?"

"I don't know. Never mind. Forget I said anything."

She knew he would not leave it alone. He never allowed her to grow quiet and uncommunicative. He told her he wanted to know what she was thinking and for her never to think that what she had to say was not important. If she had something on her mind, he wanted to hear it. He wanted to share in her thoughts, as much as she would allow him. He promised never to close himself off from her, and hoped she would promise him the same.

"Galia, tell me," he encouraged. He put his hand under her chin and gently raised her face, so their eyes met.

"I was wondering when you were going to ask me to have sex with you," there, she had said it.

"Why would you be so concerned about that, Galia? I would never disrespect you or our relationship by asking you to have sex with me. As much as I would love to make love to you, I believe it is for the confines of marriage," he looked deeply into her eyes.

That was the day he proposed and made her the envy of every girl in the dorm. She was engaged to become Mrs. Phineas Fitzhugh and she did not have to have to "put out" to get him to ask. Other girls wanted to be married and they hoped the boys they were having a sexual relationship with would feel obligated to ask them. Many of them, if not all, were sorely disappointed. They had given up their virginity to guys that never said they loved them. They hated her and she could not have been happier.

Phineas moved to Galena the summer after the proposal. He found a nice little house and asked her to help him decorate it, since it would be their home after they were married. Her parents loved him. Her father could tell that he was a decent and hardworking young man. Her mother was excited to be planning the wedding of her only daughter. Her brothers were a little hard on Phineas, at first, but quickly engrafted him into the fold. Galia could not have been happier than she felt at that moment in her life.

Who would have thought that she would be standing in the mayor's mansion of the town of her birth? As she walked out of the bathroom and into the master suite, she felt more blessed that she imagined she should feel. So many women were looking for a glimpse of the happiness she shared with Phineas. It was not because he was the mayor of the town. They had a deep-seated joy that permeated their lives from the moment they were married. Their life, together, was filled with its vicissitudes just as any other marriage. However, their pact to be open and honest with one another (and their willingness to honor the promise) has really paid off. When things get tough they speak their mind, with respect for each other's opinion, which leaves the air clear between them.

The year she dubbed, "the great darkness" was one of the hardest fought times in their marriage. They had been married for three years and Galia had become pregnant. The couple was elated. Their parents were overjoyed at the thought of becoming grandparents. She was in the early part of her eighth month and everything had been going so well with the pregnancy. Phineas had fixed up the nursery and his parents had sent a trunk full of baby clothes, diapers and other novelties. She was on her way home from work, one evening, and a drunk driver ran the stoplight and crashed into her car, on the driver's side. She felt a searing pain in her abdomen and she realized she was pinned between the door and the armrest. As she was losing consciousness, she could hear the blaring sound of the rescue squad's siren.

When she awoke in the hospital, she immediately felt her stomach. It was much smaller than she remembered. She thought it was because she had been lying down, so she tried to sit up. There was a sharp pain in her side when she moved. A nurse was at her side, advising that she lie back down. She had a couple of broken ribs that was causing the pain. The nurse told her that she had lost quite a bit of blood after the car accident. Galia could not remember the accident. Her only concern was that her baby was all right. The nurse took her by the hand and explained that the accident caused a placental abruption; this meant that the placenta had separated from the wall of her uterus. The baby was deprived of oxygen for too long and they were unable to save her.

Her... she had a daughter and her daughter had died before she could meet her. *Her...* she had a little baby girl; the baby girl that she had dreamed about. *Her...* the words echoed in her heart so loudly that it caused her physical pain. The heart monitor began to beep rapidly, and the nurse urged her to try to calm down. *Her...* did her baby's heart beat, at all? Galia's breaths were becoming shallow. She felt lightheaded. *Her...* shouldn't she be with her baby girl; a little girl needs her mother. *Her...* did she have red hair like Phineas? The darkness fell and Galia was relieved.

The year that followed the accident and death of their daughter put a strain on their promise to never grow silent. Galia could not find the meaning of words. She should be speaking softly and listening to the coos and cries of her baby girl; instead, there was a deafening silence in the nursery. The nursery she spent most of her time in, once she came home from the hospital empty-handed. She was there, when her breasts began to lactate milk that was supposed to be for their daughter. She could not find the words to describe or explain what was going on inside her mind, when she held bottles under her nipples to avoid wasting her baby's milk. She could not find the words to talk about how she had failed her baby. How she had not protected her or kept her safe from the bad people in the world. What was there to say?

Phineas was going through his own private hell, during 'the great darkness.' He had lost his baby girl and he was in fear of losing his wife. He sat in the lounge chair, across from Galia, and cried. He wanted to talk to her about the disappointment that shrouded his heart. He wanted to talk to her about the ache and emptiness that permeated everything. He wanted to hear his wife speak of her immense pain. He could not imagine what was going through her mind, and he wanted to share those moments with her. She should not be alone; neither should he. Therefore, he just sat with her and waited. He refused the offers from other women to talk about the loss of their baby. He refused their offers to console him, during this great sadness. His only consolation was to come from his beloved wife. So, he waited. He watched her because there was a time when he thought she would hurt herself.

He tried to talk to her, every day. He spoke of his love for her. He spoke of the times they had shared together. He spoke of work. He spoke about the weather. He spoke about the dinners that he was eating alone. He would not allow the silence to win. He knew she was not ready, but he would not let the quiet take over their lives. He held her in his arms, as she cried. He caressed her faced and kissed the tears, until they dried. He carried her to the shower and washed her when she did not have the strength to do it herself. In addition, he prayed.

Galia smiled at the memory, now. His voice kept her from succumbing to the silent death that beckoned her. She looked into his eyes, looking for meaning, and one day she found it. She saw his love for her and it pulled her out of the abyss. It happened, slowly, but she kept looking into his eyes and listening to his voice. She gained strength from him and the words of prayer he spoke on her behalf. She rallied herself because she wanted him and his love.

"Phineas, our baby girl is dead."

"Yes, Galia, she is."

It was a start. A seed had taken root and was beginning to grow. She went to the church for counseling because she needed some help making sense of life after the death of their daughter. They went to couple's counseling because they needed help finding their way back to one another after such an egregious tragedy. She desired her husband. She did not want the fear of pregnancy and loss to keep her away from him. She deserved to experience his love without being afraid. Zeke and Ziva Montgomery, the couple's counselors at the church, advised that their union would be healing, if she allowed it to be. God would help her with the fear, if she really wanted to be free. Making love would be an act of faith, understanding that their oneness, in God, was more powerful than the grief that surrounded them. They were right.

After Galia dressed and styled her hair, she left the house to head for work at the Galena Public Library.

CHAPTER FIVE

The short five-minute drive to work allowed Galia time, each day, to quietly greet everyone in the library. She enjoyed seeing the children come in, during the summer, to complete their summer reading assignments. Today was no disappointment. The kids always flocked toward a small section when they came in. She walked over to find Marissa Montgomery and Katriel Palmer sitting together, each with a book in hand.

"Good morning," Galia whispered to the two of them.

"Hello, Mrs. Fitzhugh," they replied in unison.

The library opened at eleven, Monday through Saturday. Galia made sure she was in by noon to set up for the afternoon reading group for the young readers and their parents. It was a program that she founded at the library ... it was her baby. She walked into her office, placed her purse in the desk drawer and took her seat. She looked at the phone. She wanted to talk to Phineas. This was the downside to the morning after; she missed him, terribly. She picked up the receiver to dial his office. She waited as the phone rang.

"The mayor's office, how may I help you?" Phyllis always sounded cordial and professional.

"Hello Phyllis, this is Galia. May I speak with the mayor?" She loved calling him that.

"Hello Galia. Yes, I will put you right through," she replied.

"Galia," Phineas spoke into the receiver.

She felt that familiar pang, in the pit of her belly, hearing his voice in her ear.

"Phineas," she answered.

Katriel used the library as a getaway from her house. The tension was palpable, even when her parents were not there. She thought their absence along with the lack of arguing and fighting would be a relief, but the stress lingered. There was no peace in their home. The old adage of 'home, sweet home' did not apply to the Palmer residence. There was nothing sweet about their family dynamic. She can see why her mother chose not to have more than one child; she would not want to have any children with her family. The thought of being in a relationship, like theirs, was abhorrent. In fact, if it had not been for the witness of the Montgomery home, she would be anti-marriage all the way. Their relationship gave her hope that men and women could reside together while maintaining a friendship and mutual respect. She was grateful, to God, for giving her such a good example because she wanted to have a family of her own. She did not want her only example to be her mother and father. She hated the energy produced by her parents. It was solemn and draining. The Montgomery's was full of energy and hope.

She believed this was why her children are so grounded, and well rounded. They were fresh and lively. Katriel felt like her energy was sullen and glum. Marissa Montgomery was her best friend and she loved her like a sister. She wanted to be a better person being around her; that was what friends were supposed to do for one another. She read more because Marissa loved to read and caused her to get excited about learning. Now, reading was a way of escape for her. She could get lost in the lives of the characters of the books and even forget what was going on around her. When she was reading books for school, she imagined herself in the story and challenged her mind to come up with resolutions or solutions to each scenario.

Marissa Montgomery was of above average height, as were her parents. Her skin was the color of honey and she had curly auburn hair. She was in honors classes, at school, and was on the road to becoming valedictorian of her graduating class. She wore a promise ring, given to her by her parents that spoke of her commitment to God and keeping herself pure for her husband. All the girls, in her class, thought her conceited because of her self-confidence. In fact, she was far from arrogant. She had insecurities like the next girl her age. The difference between her and most girls was that she did not meditate on negative things or dwell on any perceived shortcoming. Her mother instilled in her the ability to choose positive thoughts and to focus on her strengths. She was also serious about her relationship with God. She read her bible and prayed often. She attributed those things to her apparent calm demeanor and her quiet sense of poise.

Marissa wanted to be just like her mother. There was no other person, on this earth, that inspired her to be a better person. She was the most elegant woman in this town and she loved God. She was not just physically attractive; she was a beautiful soul. She was a shining example to the women of The Wisdom Outreach Center, both young and old. She respected her husband. She was a woman of prayer. She counseled women from all walks of life, without judging them. When things are not going as planned, she takes a deep breath and adjusts to the way things head. No one is perfect. Ziva Montgomery makes mistakes and has her moments of disappointment that causes her to doubt, from time to time. When that happens, she goes on a fast to get back on track. She turns off the television, she does not answer the phone, and she forfeits all forms of social media. She shuts the world out, except her family, and she communes with God.

"Beowulf is not the easiest read," Katriel whispered.

"I remember when we had to read that, last year. It was a tough one to get through. I was so relieved when Beowulf mortally wounded Grendel," Marissa hinted.

"Go Beowulf!" Katriel cheered, quietly. "What are you reading this summer?"

"Crime and Punishment," Marissa answered. "So far, in the book there's a lad named Raskolnikov who plots to murder the owner of a pawn shop. Alyona Ivanovna, the proprietor, has a mentally challenged half-sister named Lizaveta. Alyona is not the nicest person, but Lizaveta is quite the opposite. I haven't gotten much further than that, though," she continued.

"It sounds more interesting than Beowulf, that's for sure," Katriel stated.

"I guess you're right. Do you ever imagine if demons are real?" Marissa questioned.

"What do you mean?"

"Like, when you read the bible and it talks about Jesus casting out demons – do you ever think that demons are still around, today?"

Katriel thought about the question. She often thought her father was possessed with something. Why else would he be so mean and angry. However, she never really gave any real credence to her musings.

"I don't know. That is a lot to digest or even think about, really."

"I know. It brings to mind so many questions; like who is susceptible to demon possession?"

"To be honest, I thought that my dad could be under some other influence, at times."

"Really, why?"

"Well, who would marry someone they are supposed to love and then treat them the way he treats my mother? I mean, seriously, what for?"

The two girls grew quiet as they pondered the idea. Marissa, silently, prayed for Katriel's father and mother. She, also, prayed for herself and her friend. She did not want to be a candidate or a welcoming committee for demons. Her mother often said, '*an idle mind is the devil's workshop.*' She wondered if that was all it took, for someone to be unfocused on something. She thought of the scripture in Isaiah chapter twenty-six, "*You will keep him in perfect peace, whose mind is stayed on You, because he trusts in you.*" Marissa vowed to be sure to keep her mind turned toward God, especially, when there was nothing to do.

There was a hushed commotion going on in the front of the library that caught the girls' attention. It was Axel Fitzhugh, the librarian's son. Marissa knew him because he went to the University of Wisconsin with her brother, Jaden. She also knew him because her parents and his parents were good friends. He was much shorter than she was, probably because both of his parents were not very tall, but he was attractive with his strawberry blonde curly locks. He had green eyes, just like his father, and freckles adorned his face like little chocolate chips. Always so laid back, nothing ever seemed to bother him. He was still undeclared, in college; something her brother did not think was a good trait. She told Jaden that not everyone went into college with all the answers. They took their first year, sometimes their sophomore, to choose a career path to follow. The fact that Axel was heading into his junior year shot holes in her summation. Nevertheless, she still thought he was cute and wished he would see her as a young woman and not the skinny little sister of his friend.

He spotted them, in the corner, and headed toward them. Marissa smoothed her hair and smiled as he drew closer.

"Hey 'Rissa," he greeted her in the nickname he gave her when she was in junior high school.

"Hey Axel," she replied.

Katriel took note of the slight blush on Marissa's face. She sat back in her seat to watch the exchange between her and Axel. He seemed very relaxed while talking, while Marissa stammered a bit and then regained her composure.

"What brings you to the library?" Marissa asked.

"Looking for my mom; have you seen her?"

"Yes, she is in her office, I believe."

"Thanks, 'Rissa," he reached over and tussled her hair.

"I hate when you do that, Axel," Marissa fussed, as she smoothed her hair back into place.

"I know, that's why I do it. Well, see ya."

"Bye," she spoke to his back, as he was already walking away.

Marissa looked over at Katriel who had not taken her eyes off her since Axel walked over.

"Interesting," Katriel stated.

"What?"

"Just how flustered you got when Axel got here."

"I know! It really bothers me that he gets under my skin the way he does. He doesn't even notice that I am a young woman, now. To him, I am still that scrawny girl with braces, from junior high school," she sighed.

"I don't see what you see in him, in the first place. He seems too laid back; like nothing matters to him."

"Yeah, but that doesn't have to be a bad thing, does it?"

Katriel shrugged her shoulders. "I don't know. I'm not sure I would be cool with someone who didn't seem to care about anything."

Marissa thought about what her friend was saying. It was true that Axel seemed to lack passion in any direction. He did not have any real likes or dislikes; he somewhat just went with the flow. She remembered hearing their parents talking, one evening, and Mr. Fitzhugh was concerned about Axel not having a clear vision for his life at his age. Her father told his father not to worry about him because he was still young. For some kids it took a little more time than others to get their footing, her father stated. She began to wonder about Axel and her mother's saying about idle minds, and a cold chill ran up her spine.

"I guess you are right, Katriel," she agreed after some time.

Ghrelin had been standing beside Axel, while he was speaking with Marissa. He was being ignored, just as Katriel had been, but he did not mind. He was used to taking a back seat to those he accompanied. It never bothered him that they never introduced them to their friends, family or acquaintances. He knew his place and he was fine with it.

He and Axel had been hanging out, since last night, not doing anything in particular and wanting more of it. Axel loved it when he had free time; it made him crave more of it. It was the reason he did not have a job, he did not want to have to be occupied. He knew it bothered his parents (especially his father) that he was not actively searching for employment now that school was out. He had been home for over a month and was enjoying his freedom. His mother and father should remember how they felt when they had a break from school. He was certain they did not want to rush into another responsibility after slaving away at the books all year long. He earned the right to veg out for a bit.

Ghrelin stood to the side, as Axel knocked on his mother's office door. He heard her give him permission to enter, so he opened the door. The two of them walked in, together. He stayed by the door as Axel got to the business at hand.

"Hey mom, I must have been asleep when you left this morning," he began.

"Axel, I thought maybe you were out on the hunt," Galia replied.

"On the hunt for what, Mom?"

"A job, Axel, what else?"

"Please, not that, again. I will get to it when I get to it. I wish you and Dad would stop harassing me about finding a job. I just got out of school, Mom. I need some breathing room," he whined.

"Seriously, Axel, breathing room? Why do you need breathing room? You barely matriculated, this semester," she added.

"I took the needed credits to stay on campus."

"Exactly, Axel, the barest minimum. I am concerned that we have not instilled any sort of work ethic in you.

"Mom, don't go there. I just came to get some money so I can go have some fun. I need to relax and get my mind off of some things."

"You have things on your mind, Axel?" Galia questioned.

"Are you going to give me the money or not?" Axel ignored her question.

"I am not going to give you any more of my hard earned money, Axel. You are a young man and you should start acting as such. Go out there, get yourself a job and make your own money."

Ghrelin and Axel sighed, in unison. Axel wanted easy money and Ghrelin supported his ideas. Why should he have to work for it when his father was the mayor and his mother the head librarian? They made plenty of money. His father would be mayor for at least another four years, giving him time to decide what he wanted to do with his life. In the meantime, he needed to convince his mother to foot his bill for today.

"Mom, please – I will not come to you about money anymore this week. I will start looking for a job, next week, I promise," he lied

Galia thought for a moment. It was hard for her to resist him for long. She reached into her desk drawer and pulled out her purse. She took out her wallet and gave Axel fifty dollars. This should tie him over until he can start that job hunt.

"You're the best, Mom," Axel kissed her cheek. "I'm going to leave you to your work."

He opened the door and quietly walked out. Ghrelin was close on his heels.

"I knew she would give in," Axel spoke.

"She always does," Ghrelin agreed. He knew that the more Axel's parents coddled him, the more free time he would crave to spend with him. He enjoyed the company and didn't want anything to get in the way of that.

CHAPTER SIX

The children played in the backyard, while Sofia Koen looked on like the doting mother. She was ecstatic that she could stay home and raise her children, while Levi worked to take care of their family. She knew there were other mothers who wish they had a husband who would allow them to be the primary caregiver for their children. Nevertheless, alas, they were less fortunate. Levi was a strong man and took his role as the head of their house seriously. She was a blessed woman, indeed.

Her good fortune bode well for Babette Richmond, as well. Her station, in life, allowed her the time to care for the Richmond children, as well. Talia, Jonah and Brayden got along with each other as well as her own children, Hannah and the twins Asher and Ahavah. There were times that she did not understand how Babette could leave her children, every day to go out and make a career for herself. She should be thinking of her children and their sense of well-being. Instead, she was self-centered and self-seeking in her choices. Sofia tried not to judge her and the other mothers in their neighborhood, but it was difficult not to do so. Just as she made the decision to choose her family over her own ambitions, any mother could have done it.

Prior to marriage and children, Sofia was a successful account executive in an upscale advertising agency in Chicago. She worked hard and made her fair share of money. She maintained a condominium in one of the most affluent neighborhoods and she shopped at the best boutiques. However, when she met Levi she began to rethink her priorities. She started thinking about what her fast-paced life would mean for family. Sure, while she and Levi dated, it was fine. He was an administrator in the school system in Galena and that kept him busy. As a couple, prior to marriage, they spent weekends together leaving the workweek to work. Their careers took front and center, as it should.

When Levi decided to ask her to marry him, Sofia immediately began to change her way of thinking. She had a two-year plan from which she began to work. Their wedding occurred on a perfect day in May. She wore the traditional white gown and they opted for the not-so-traditional Jewish marriage ceremony. Both parents were disappointed, but it was short-lived. The fact that she waited until she was twenty-seven years old was an embarrassment to her mother. In the end, her mother was happy she was not going to be a spinster, and she had hopes of becoming a bubby.

According to her plan, she and Levi would enjoy one another's company for a year, and then begin to have children. By that time, she will have lightened her load enough, at work, to put in her notice. She was grateful that her husband agreed with her plan as they implemented a savings plan that would leave them comfortable and not put a strain on their finances. They had accrued a decent nest egg by the time she was ready to leave her job. They calculated their spending, including monthly debt as well as any frivolous spending. By the time they had Hannah, two years later, they had saved a year's worth of spending as a nest egg. They paid their mortgage twice a month, in an attempt to reduce their debt from thirty years to fifteen. They paid all of their household expenses ahead for several months while she was still working. Therefore, when she came off her job, they were set for many years to come.

If they could do it, other families could do it. The Richmonds did not have any excuse. Both Cale and Babette have great jobs; he is a circuit court judge for Jo Daviess County and she is a real estate lawyer at one of the top law firms, in Galena. Together they had to make close to four-hundred thousand dollars a year, Sofia estimated. They certainly did pay her well to care for their three beautiful children. The money she received from the Richmonds allowed for her to take care of her personal desires, like spa days and going to the hairdresser.

Mavet sat down next to Sofia on the lounge chair. He enjoyed her company and she enjoyed his. They were able to talk about things that she felt Levi would not understand. He did not think he was better than the other husbands whose wives worked. He knew it was a personal choice that they made and other families made choices that worked for them. Mavet, on the other hand, agreed with her about working mothers and the husbands that refuse to take their rightful places within the family. He never grew tired of listening to her go on and on about Babette Richmond and her selfish ways. He even tossed in, from time to time, that African American women were different from Jewish women. They cut from a different cloth and their ideals were off kilter. She was not ready to entertain such prejudicial thinking, but she had no problem with judging people's actions.

She was quick to pit her family values up against those that did not line up with her way of thinking. In her mind, if no one did things the way she did, or think about things in the same manner as she did, then they were wrong. She knew her way was the best way … just look at her children and how well adjusted they were. They were well behaved, socially adept especially for their ages. She shook her head every time Babette brought the children over to the house. The Richmond children were good children; however, Sofia attributed much of that to her influence in their lives. She could not fathom that their mother had time to instill any good qualities into them just being a weekend mom. Their well-roundedness had to be because they spent so much time with her and her children, because they certainly did not spend much time with their own family.

Sofia looked at her watch and realized it was time to take the kids to the Reading Circle Group at the public library. She was so grateful to see that Galena had a children's reading group just like the one she had researched in Chicago prior to making the decision to move here. It was important for her to expose her children to as many books as she could because it would lay the perfect foundation for learning once they attended school.

"Hannah, Asher, Ahavah, Talia, Jonah and Brayden get your things it is time for the reading group," she called.

They all gathered up the toys and put them in their proper place before heading into the house to wash their hands and get a snack. Once the table cleared and the trash discarded, they walked out to the minivan in the driveway. Sofia buckled the smaller ones into their car seats, while the other children fastened their seatbelts. She got into the driver's seat and closed the door. Mavet took his seat on the passenger side of the car. As she adjusted the rear view mirror, she ensured the children were comfortable and ready to go. She backed, slowly, out of the driveway and headed toward the library.

Sofia and Mavet conversed while the children talked amongst themselves, on the short trip to

Galena Public Library. She was hoping that the twins did not fall asleep before arriving because they awakened early this morning. She checked the mirror. They were smiling at Hannah's attempt to entertain them. She smiled and told Mavet that she was lucky to have such beautiful children. She wished that her mother had taken the time with her and her siblings. Mavet listened intently as she bemoaned childhood and her desperation to escape from it. She knew there was a better way and she worked very hard to make that happen. She busied herself around the house to insure it continued to run smoothly. She made sure that Levi had everything he needed to be the success he desired. She worked in the children's ministry at the Wisdom Outreach Center. She was on the women's ministry and she was part of the intercessory team. She led a very full, productive life and she ran her home like a well-oiled machine.

She pulled the minivan into a parking space. She was lucky to have found something very close to the door. She and Mavet exited the vehicle. She unbuckled the small ones, insured the older children were out of the car and on the sidewalk. She pushed the 'lock' button on the keyless remote and encouraged the children to hold hands as they walked inside. She reminded them that they are to use their inside voices while inside the library. Sofia told them they are going to listen to Mrs. Fitzhugh read a very exciting story.

Everyone was looking at how well behaved the children were, as they walked into the library. Sofia could hear the whispers of awe as she walked to the children's reading room. She smiled within. She would be sure to tell Babette how impressed the people were with her children's manners, today. Levi would also get a report on the children. Mavet patted her on the back, telling her she is doing an excellent job as usual.

"Good afternoon Mrs. Fitzhugh," Sofia spoke as she walked into the center. Sofia noticed that she was the first of the parents to arrive. In reality, not many mothers actually brought their children. She realized that daycare providers, both public and private, were the main participants. She shook her head.

"Good afternoon Mrs. Koen. So glad to see you, again," Galia smiled and shook her hand. "As usual, the children follow the library rules to the letter. You are doing a wonderful service to your children and the Richmond children, as well."

"Thank you, Mrs. Fitzhugh. I do my best," she stated demurely.

"There are some older mothers who would love to know your secret."

"Well, I am no different than any other mother, Mrs. Fitzhugh. It just takes time and dedication."

"I am sure you are right."

Sofia and Mavet looked at each other. Of course, she was right. The fact that some mothers did not want to take the time was the real issue. Just as she had done, making her family the most important priority, they could have made the same choices. She smiled as she watched the children take their seats and patiently wait for story time to begin. Asher and Ahavah began swinging their legs and talking to one another. She walked over to them and leaned in closely to tell them that was not the appropriate behavior.

"They are fine, Ms. Koen," Galia stated.

Sofia felt herself getting angry at the interruption. No one should be telling her what acceptable behavior is for her children. She was their mother and she was not going to tolerate the twins acting out like the others she saw while out in public. She calmed herself before speaking.

"It would not be fine, Mrs. Fitzhugh, if they were required to sit still and remain quiet while in school. I just want them to practice good social behaviors now, so as to not be challenged when they are away from me," Sofia answered.

Galia could sense a note of hostility in Sofia's tone and backed off. She remembered how impatient this mother could be and intolerant of any childish behavior. She made a note to pray for the Koen kids. The pressure put on them, by their mother, would make it difficult for them to not be critical of others. Yet, every household is different and Galia had to keep that in mind. It was not her place to advise or correct, so she just moved on to the next task at hand.

As the other children came into the room, there were hushed conversations taking place all around. Sofia had a look of disdain on her face, as she talked with Mavet. They agreed that the children should have known better than to carry on conversation in a library. She shook her head, as she watched the caretakers sit and allow this type of behavior to continue.

"It is time to begin, children," Galia started. The room grew quiet, as the children turned to face her. "As is our custom, we are going to start with one of Aesop's fables. For those who come often, you know this is the time where we learn good life lessons through a simple story. Today's fable is called, '*The Jay and the Peacock.*'"

Galia went on to tell the children how the blue jay crossed the fence into a yard full of peacocks. He noticed there were some of the peacock's feathers on the ground because they were molting. The blue jay thought it would be good to strut around like a peacock and be like one of them. So, he tied some of the feathers to himself and began walking with them. When the peacocks realized that the blue jay was a fraud, they plucked the feathers from him, and he left the yard to return to the other jays. Galia let the children know that the blue jay's friends were not very happy with him, either, because it appeared that he was dissatisfied with himself...his true self.

The children were listening intently. Galia knew they loved to hear about any type of animal, which is why she chose this particular fable, today.

"Can anyone tell me what they think the moral of the story is?" Galia asked.

Talia Richmond raised her hand and Galia called her name.

"The moral of the story is that it is best to be happy with whom you are and not try to pretend to be like someone else," the eight year old recited, with confidence.

Sofia was ecstatic. She felt like her influence was making an impact on the little girl.

"My mother always tells us that it is important to be grateful for the person God made us," Talia added.

Mavet quickly turned his head toward Sofia. He could see the smoldering look on her face, as the child gave credit to her mother and not to Sofia.

Sofia was offended. Of all the things she could have thought to say that she had done to instill good morals, she choose to give her mother credit for something. The mother who was at work, and not home raising her own children, could not have really taught her anything. In fact, it was not the ideal thing for her to be telling her children, in the first place. The Richmond children really could learn a thing or two about proper guidance. In addition, to give God credit for making them... how preposterous does that sound? It is the parents, mothers mainly, that shape and mold children into the people they are going to become when they are adults. The bible clearly states to bring up a child in the way that they should go and when they are old, they will not depart from it – that is the job of the parents, not God.

"Well, your mother is a smart woman for teaching you that," Galia stated.

"My mother is a smart lady," Jonah added. His little round face shone with pride.

Not very smart overfeeding you, Sofia mutter under her breath. Mavet smirked at her comment.

The other caretakers and Galia chuckled at his comment, but not Sofia. She sat glaring at them as if they had spat out profanity. No one in the room missed her disapproving stare.

CHAPTER SEVEN

The police room was in an uproar with the latest news of a missing person, which everyone in town has presumed dead. The chief of police, Gavin Palmer, was barking out commands and sending out officers to continue to search the area where the person was last seen. The news spread quickly, as the Galena Gazette had run the story front page of the paper for the last six days. Maddock Hamilton, a Caucasian male, weighing approximately one hundred eighty pounds, had been training for the Chicago Marathon when he had gone missing off one of the Galena River Trails, a week ago. His girlfriend, Samantha Redman, reported the incident to the police when he did not return from his run. She was hysterical, which always annoyed Gavin. He hated emotionally draining women. It took too much energy to calm her down, which sapped his patience and sent him into a tirade.

"Just tell me what happened," he yelled.

She sniffled and cried. She whimpered and stammered. He felt his blood rushing to his head and causing it to pulsate. He did not need a headache to add to his day.

"Ma'am, we will be unable to help you if you cannot get the words out," Officer Gray Jenkins calmly spoke. He cut his eye at the Chief and then returned his attention to the distraught woman.

That was a week ago and they were no closer to solving this mystery than they were when the sniveling woman came into the department. Gavin despised long, drawn out cases on his docket. Therefore, he had to get involved to get this cleared up. Gray and his partner, Officer Etmus Sadiyo, were great cops. He assigned them to the investigation when he saw how Gray had calmed Samantha down enough to speak coherently. He knew the dynamic duo, as they liked to be called, would quickly gather some leads to get things moving. It was not the case. Every lead had led to a dead end. There was literally no trace of Maddock Hamilton, anywhere. It was as if he simply vanished.

Gray and Etmus went to the Galena River Trail about an hour after they talked with the girlfriend. They looked around at the head of the trail, because that is where Maddock would have had to return. The team noticed a gold Toyota Avalon parked in the parking lot. They took a picture of it, thinking it could have been the missing person's automobile. There were footprints and bicycle tire tracks, all along the trail. The path was for bikers, hikers, runners and walkers.

As the police officers walked the trail, they noticed there were low-lying tree limbs that were broken off. As they looked closer, they saw what could have been evidence of a struggle. Along with the broken tree limbs, there were uprooted shrubs; there were leaves that appeared disturbed, and created a pathway, which could be from dragging someone. They snapped pictures and continued to follow the lead. In the end, it just proved to be a vulture that moved a badger through the forested area.

When the two returned to the precinct they called Samantha Redman to ask what kind of car, Maddock Hamilton drove. She confirmed it was a gold colored Avalon. The picture posted to an evidence board at the station. Samantha agreed to meet Gray and Etmus at Galena River Trail with a spare key to search the car for clues. After searching the car, they were no closer to solving the mystery than they had been the day before.

They questioned people at Maddock's job, at his favorite hangout spots and the people of the church he attended, the Wisdom Outreach Center. Gray understood why this case got under Gavin's skin, as he was a member of the same church. The victim also ran along the same trails that his daughter, Katriel, frequented with her friends. The pressure was mounting as each day passed with no resolution. The chief's fuse was getting shorter and shorter. Gray knew his friend well. It would not be long before everyone would begin to feel the fire of Gavin's fury.

Today seemed to be the day. Gavin Palmer was in rare form. He ranted and raved about everything. There was no consoling him. Worry and upset creased his face. The mayor's office was calling constantly inquiring on the status of the case. The reporter, Lynda Sky, seemed to sleep at the station. She was ever present, asking questions and making notes on her iPad. He wished he could command her to leave, but the precinct was open to the public. Besides, it would not be good for the community to have bad press about the police trying to hide something. Therefore, he brewed. He needed a break in the case; and he needed it yesterday.

"Jenkins and Sadiyo," Gavin barked.

Gray and Etmus rose from their desks and walked into the chief's office. They closed the door behind them and took a seat, in front of his desk.

"What the hell is going on with this case?" Gavin's frustration was evident in his voice and demeanor.

"Well, Chief," Etmus began, "We are coming up empty at every turn. This man had no enemies, he had a good relationship with his longstanding girlfriend and he was a member in good standing at the Wisdom Outreach Center. He had a good job here in Galena, and he was training for the Chicago Marathon."

"Have we contacted the Chicago police department?" Gavin asked.

"Yes, we have," Gray chimed in. "They have posted a missing person's report in every district there, as well."

"You know the Gazette is sensationalizing this whole thing and that reporter has the community in an uproar," Gavin hissed.

"We are aware of the mounting concern from the public."

"I am getting flack from the parishioners at the church, as well. It is getting on my damn nerves. My wife, daughter and everyone else are looking at me to do something. And now, I am looking at the two of you."

Mavet sat in the corner watching the scenario play out in front of him. He and Gavin had been talking prior to him calling the two officers to his office. He allowed the chief to rant, rave and place blame. He fired back giving him license for his anger. Mavet knew how incompetent his crew was and how it seemed like no one was doing his job. He told Gavin that he understood how the pressure was mounting at work and how he needed a break when he was home. Nora and Katriel should understand, as well. They were the ones who knew him best; knew what he demanded and expected. Yet, they were chiming in with everyone else, asking him more questions than he had answers. In fact, when Nora called this morning, Gavin exploded, leaving his wife in tears as he slammed down the phone.

"Gavin, what are you going to do about all of this?" Mavet asked. "Why can't anyone see that you need a competent team if this town is to be protected and this case is to get solved?"

"What good is it for me to have, who I thought to be, my best men on the case and still have no answers?" Gavin was speaking to Gray and Etmus. He stared them in the faces, waiting for a response.

"Chief, we are doing …"

"You are doing nothing!" Gavin interrupted. "You get out there and comb through that trail until you find something. Do not come back to this precinct until you have Maddock in tow, dead or alive."

The two men rose from their seats and walked out of the door, closing it behind them. Gray looked at Etmus and shrugged his shoulders. The both of them were well aware of the pressure that that a precinct often faces when cases are not solved quickly. They had loved ones looking to them for answers and resolution just like the chief. It did not matter to the women in their lives that they were not in charge. They were of the fraternal order; and everyone expected the force to get the job done. However, when it came to the mayor's office and the Gazette, the onus of the situation fell fully onto the shoulders of the chief of police. They knew they had to make him look good by getting some answers to this mystery. They tidied up their desks and headed out of the door, with everyone in the squad room looking at their backs.

Mavet and Gavin sat in his office trying to make sense of what was going on, in this case. Why were there so many loose ends and very little clues? All they had was Maddock's car and very little else. They did not have a real crime scene, and the thought of having to inspect the more than three miles of forested area was a nightmare. All sorts of animals roamed the trail. There were vagabonds that camped out near the railroad tracks and along the backside of the Mississippi River. Anyone could have done anything to Maddock Hamilton and no one would ever find out. He did not want to start dragging the river, but Gavin was beginning to think he did not have an option.

"You may have to go down there yourself, Gavin," Mavet offered.

Gavin sighed. He had done his fair share of getting his shoes dirty with cases like this before he became chief. He hated walking the beat, interacting with the community and having someone breathing down his neck because he was not moving according to their expectations. Once he was the one in charge, he had settled within himself that he would not be out on the beat, again. Yet, here he was, faced with having to make this decision. He did not want the daunting task of asking questions and pulling the pieces together from people's disjointed thoughts. He did not want to do it.

"You are going to have to do it. No one else cares about your reputation," Mavet advised. "This is your neck on the line, as far as the mayor's office is concerned."

"Dammit!" Gavin exclaimed.

He opened his desk drawer and grabbed his holster. After strapping it to himself, he stormed out of the office. All of the officers looked astounded as Gavin walked past them, in a huff, and headed out of the door behind the other two officers. Mavet was nearby. He would ride in the squad car with Gavin as they headed toward Depot Park. Once the two cars arrived, Etmus, Gray and Gavin stood in the parking area. They all agreed that while the partners started on this end, Gavin would start at the back end by South Galena Junction. Mavet followed Gavin back to his car and they headed toward US 20 Highway Bridge.

The longer he drove, the angrier he became. There was no reason he should be out in the field. He knew he could be of more use back at the station, but he had to get some answers. He heard the familiar crackle of the police radio. It was the operator calling for his car. He picked up the receiver and answered.

"This is car 50, Gavin speaking," he spoke into the hand-held.

"We just received a call from someone who refused to give his name stating he believes he sees a body down between the river and the old railroad tracks in the Galena Trails," the operator advised.

"And why the hell are you calling me and not sending someone out, directly?" Gavin yelled.

"Sir, they asked specifically for you to come," the operator calmly replied.

Gavin and Mavet looked at one another. How would someone know who was headed in that direction, at this very moment? Moreover, why this man would be asking for the chief of police to come out to what could be a crime scene, is baffling. The proper protocol was to call the station and for any free officer to head out on the call. What was going on in this town?

He slammed his hands on the steering wheel, turned on his siren, and headed toward the backside of the Mississippi River by the old railroad tracks. It did not take long for them to arrive at the scene and what greeted them shook Gavin to the core. He put his foot on the brake, pushed the gear into the park position and slowly got out of the car. He pulled his gun and walked cautiously ahead. The sky was dark with birds of prey and there seemed to be something lying in the marsh by the river. The noise was unbearable. He could not understand how the lone figure could be standing so close to the commotion and not have to cover his ears. It was deafening.

"This is the police," Gavin yelled, yet his voice was muffled by the eerie shrill of the birds.

He turned from left to right, and then back again. There was a chill in the air, even though it was June. Gavin sensed a sudden movement to his left. He turned, quickly. There was nothing. The sound was coming from his right, now. He turned, again. There was nothing. The flapping of the birds' wings and their screeching was unnerving. He walked further, slowly. His senses were on high alert. All of a sudden, the dead leaves, from many years of autumns, began to swirl around as if a mighty wind had picked up. Dust, debris and natural compost flew around Gavin's face. His eyes became gritty and his mouth filled with the flying matter. He swiped at his head, attempting to shield himself from the fragments.

"Gavin," the wind seemed to scream his name.

He coughed and coughed, trying to clear his throat from the rubbish that was churning around him.

"I've been waiting for this moment, Gavin," the wind spoke, again.

Gavin tried to see through the darkness. He wanted to know who or what was talking to him, in the midst of such turmoil. He tried to get angry, but fear was coming up instead.

"Isn't this what you wanted, Gavin?"

"I don't know what you are talking about," he coughed.

"You wanted commotion and turmoil in the lives of those around you."

"That is crazy," he coughed. Now, Gavin could feel the anger replacing the fear. He did not appreciate what was going on. It seemed like some stunt and he was going to find the underlying cause of this. He could see, vaguely, the figure of the man still standing by the river's edge. He was looking at him, too. His eyes seemed to shine in their sockets.

"I gave you everything you wanted, Gavin," it seemed as if the voice was emanating from within the man's eyes.

"What the hell are you talking about, you loon?" Gavin yelled.

"You sought reasons to be angry."

"I did what?" Gavin was trying to walk through the tumult. He wanted to get to this man and put his hands around his throat.

In an instant, the winds died down and the debris fell back to the ground. When Gavin straightened up, the man was standing in front of him. He was surprised at the speed in which the man traversed the space between them. Before he knew it, he was grabbed up into a vice grip. He could not move. He tried to struggle against the hold, but his efforts were futile. He raised his gun to shoot, but it was slung to the ground by some inhuman force. Anger rose to monumental heights, within Gavin. He began to swell with fury and he welled up a guttural bellow from the depths of his being. A hand wrapped around his throat and began to squeeze. It squeezed until the yelling could no longer be heard through the trees.

"What was that?" Gray asked Etmus as they walked through the trail.

"I don't know but it sounded like it came from the direction of the river," Etmus answered.

"You think it was some animal?"

"It sure did sound beastly."

The two officers began to run toward the sound. When they approached the river's edge, they stopped in their tracks.

CHAPTER EIGHT

Jarhys Houston would not describe himself as an attractive man. In fact, if someone asked him how he would rank amongst other men, on a scale from one to ten, he would say a solid six or seven. He did not live a world of self-deception; he knew his physical appearance would not win him any awards. Yet, his confidence was through the roof. In addition, he was a strong and virile man. What he lacked in good looks, he superseded in intellect and charisma. He could charm the panties off any woman, one of his college buddies once said. It was true, he must confess. There was never a shortage of women vying for his attention. He stood slightly over six feet tall, with a very masculine build; strong, broad shoulders which tapered down to a small waist. His legs were long and muscular, his voice a deep baritone. He accentuated his body with tailored suits and custom-made shoes. It did not hurt that he was one of the highest paid African American lawyers in Dubuque, Iowa. Although he lived in Galena, it made financial sense to ply his trade in a more metropolitan area.

He grabbed a towel from the linen closet, in his upstairs hallway, and then headed toward the personal gym housed in the basement of his three-thousand square foot home. He did not have the time to go to a public gym to jockey for equipment or compete with other men's insecurities. His body was a work of art that required constant maintenance and he could not be at the whim of some insignificant man who was working out for fun. He catered to his body, like a fine woman. He fed it the best foods. He kept himself well hydrated and he worked out six days a week, leaving Sundays free to relax and attend the Wisdom Outreach Center. His work schedule could be very harrowing and he needed a day to rejuvenate the soul. He admired Pastor Zeke. He looked like a man that cared about his appearance, as much as he did. He could not say that he ascribed to everything he preached, but he was an articulate orator and a learned man. In addition, his wife was *fine*.

He smiled, to himself, as he thought about the porcelain doll that warmed his bed from time to time. Winter Pharron was a beauty. She worked hard, had a good head on her shoulders and she was a spitfire in the courtroom. He loved to watch her strut her stuff, in front of the jury. Her blonde hair was cut close to her head in a flattering bob. She wore dark glasses, a stark contrast to her alabaster skin. She was slender and petite with just the right amount of fat in the right places. She matched his passion for the finer things, in life. She took time to pamper her body and he appreciated that. What he loved most about Winter was her independence. She was not needy and clingy, like some women. She knew what she wanted and was willing to do what was necessary to get it.

Jarhys had not been one of those brothers who sought out vanilla ice cream. He had been a loyal chocolate lover, since he could remember. Not that there were not enough of them clamoring for him, he just did not indulge. Winter introduced him to the idea of entertaining the thought of what it would be like to sample her flavor. She sauntered into the practice, one day, after being brought on by one of the partners. She had been with a firm in Chicago, but had relocated to Galena to get away from the hustle and bustle of the busy city life. He had been hard at work, with his paralegal, because he had a big upcoming case. He did not give her a glance, until she had passed his office. Her fragrance caught his attention. He was stopped, mid-sentence, by the very feminine scent. He looked up, just as she was passing by, and his interest further piqued by the round bottom he saw swaying past his door.

He rose from his desk and walked out of his office to see where she headed. Just before she turned into the office, two doors down, their eyes met. She flashed a dazzling smile, winked her eye and continued through the door after Roger Thurman, a partner. He stood there, pondering her gesture for a moment longer, then returned to his desk and the task at hand. He would have to introduce himself at another time; right now, he had business to take care of and no time to waste. It was several days later, before he would have the pleasure of making her acquaintance.

Jarhys put the towel on the elliptical machine. He punched in the settings so he would start out on a moderate run, to warm up his body. He put in his headphones and began his workout to the sound of Anthony Hamilton. He closed his eyes and began to meditate on his goals. He envisioned himself at the top of his game, in every aspect of his life. He saw life going exactly as planned. He was very close to making partner, in the firm. As the music played, he moved from circuit to circuit on the machine. After forty-five minutes, he moved to the weight bench. He would do ten reps of eight with thirty pounds, and then move to eight reps of eight with forty pounds. As he was moving to his third and final circuit with the weights, eight reps of eight at fifty pounds, his cell phone rang. He let it go to voicemail. He would have to return the call because he nearing the end of his workout.

Once completed, he toweled dry and finished with sixteen ounces of coconut water. He grabbed his phone and headed upstairs. He swiped the screen to see whose call he had missed. It was Winter. He smiled, to himself. It was time for her Jarhys fix. It was almost as if she had him penciled in for every three days. It did not matter when that third day fell - during the week, on the weekends or holidays. Winter was going to have her some Jarhys. He laughed aloud at his folly. He dialed her number.

"Hello, Winter," his baritone voice was mellow as he spoke into the receiver.

"Jarhys, I need you," Winter stated, softly.

"I just finished my workout and I am heading to the shower," he offered.

She knew when she called and he advised he headed for the showers, that he was inviting her to his place. It never failed; by the time he was finished grooming, she was ringing his bell.

"I will be right over," she whispered in his ear and she hung up the phone.

Jarhys knew it would take her approximately thirty minutes to get to his house from her home. He headed straight to the bathroom and let the rain showerhead erase the evidence of a workout from his body. He felt revitalized and ready to handle Winter's needs. She would handle his, as well. They were a perfect match in their passions, in the courtroom and in the bedroom. He knew he would require another shower before he went to bed for the night, but that was par for the course. He was willing to put in the work, as it was well worth it.

Thirty minutes after the call he heard Winter's car pull into his driveway. He walked down the stairs in nothing but his boxer shorts. He waited for her to ring the bell; he did not want to appear anxious. Once she pushed the button, he unlocked the door to find her standing on his steps in a sheer negligee that was the color of merlot wine and Christian Louboutin shoes. Her makeup was impeccable and her creamy skin glistened in the moonlight. Jarhys felt the blood coursing through his body and cause his manhood to stiffen. She walked passed him and he closed the door behind her. The scent of her filled his nostrils and he lifted her off her feet and headed up the stairs.

He laid her on the bed and she parted her legs. His mouth greeted her with such ardor that her breath arrested in her chest. She arched her back, moaning as his warm tongue circled and swirled like a hummingbird at a flower. Jarhys was a salacious lover and Winter met his fervor. She stretched her arms out wide and grabbed the sheet as he took her higher and higher. Her heart was racing and her body was on fire. She needed him deep inside her. She reached down and pulled him into her, welcoming his full eight inches. She threw her head back, in abandon, and screamed his name.

They lay spent, on the bed, after an hour of wanton sexual pleasure. Winter still had on her shoes, but the negligee was thrown onto the chair across the room. Jarhys let his finger lightly caress her exposed nipple and a soft sigh escaped her lips. They basked in the aftermath of their passion like intimate lovers. They spoke of their day and the upcoming court cases. Both of them had to appear before the Honorable Cale Richmond, during the upcoming week in Jo Daviess County Courthouse. The Judge was hard, but fair. It required their best work if they dared hope of winning a case in his court.

Before long, the two of them walked down the stairs and into the kitchen. They had worked up quite an appetite and they needed a snack. Jarhys went to the refrigerator while Winter took a seat on the stool, at the counter. She swung her legs as he heated up a vegan style chili he made the night before. Her skin looked aglow in the soft amber lights. She lifted her leg to rest her foot on the cool granite. He walked over, removed her shoes, and kissed her polished toes. He ran his tongue across the arch of her foot, as his hands slid up her leg. He felt himself rise, again. He reached under her bottom to scoop her up and onto his engorged erection. In the same moment, they heard a cell phone ringing in the foyer. Winter had allowed her purse to slip from her arm when he lifted her.

"Dammit," she whispered. "I've got to get that."

Jarhys placed her onto the floor and she went to retrieve the phone before the ringing could stop.

"Hello, Gray," she answered, attempting to erase the sultriness from her voice. "I see that you made it home. I will be there, just as soon as I can. I left your dinner, in the microwave. Yes, baby. I love you, too."

She hung up the phone and walked back into the kitchen. "It was Gray," she stated, in a matter of fact tone.

"Yes, I figured, as much," Jarhys replied.

"Now, where were we?" She hopped back on the stool and invited him in.

After they sated their appetites, they headed back to the bedroom and into the shower. Winter could not go home to Gray with the scent of Jarhys on her body. She had the slightest pang of guilt at the fact that she did not want to use protection when she was with him. If Gray ever wanted to make love to her after she left Jarhys, she made sure that he did not put his mouth to her. In fact, she preferred Jarhys to her own man, when it came to that department. His level of expertise far exceeded that of her live-in boyfriend.

She reached into her bag and pulled out a pair of jeans and a t-shirt. She rarely wore panties and she didn't need a bra. She placed the negligee into the purse and sprayed her signature scent onto her naked skin before putting on the clothes. She hired a perfumer to create this scent, named 'Winter', especially made for her. It took several attempts before he matched the fragrance with the chemistry of her body. He was able to capture and enhance her unique pheromone composition. She knew it had an overwhelming effect on Jarhys; this is the reason she sprays it in his bedroom after their sessions and before she leaves. The psychological effect of scent and memory were not lost to her. She knew her scent would always remind him of their moments and he would long for her just as she longed for him.

Jarhys was not naïve to what Winter was doing when she marked her territory, for the night, with her scent. He did not care. He was enraptured with the fragrance; he had been since the day she walked into the firm. He welcomed it. He knew he left an indelible imprint on her sexual psyche, as well. They were irresistible to one another; this is why they stayed away from one another in the office. If she senses his closeness, it puts her in heat. If he gets a full whiff of her fragrance, he cannot conceal his desire. When the third day approaches, they have their secretaries plan a power lunch in downtown Dubuque. They do not leave at the same time, neither return with one another. They simply meet at the Hilton where Jarhys has a private suite for nights when court runs late and he does not feel like driving back to Galena.

Winter and Jarhys walked back down the stairs. She kissed him full on the lips before she opened the door to leave. He watched as her hips swayed on the way to her car. She got into the car and pulled out of the driveway. He closed the door and headed back to his bedroom. There was still work to be done before he went to bed for the night. He smiled, as he smelled the air. He knew she would call him, once she reached her garage. Although they were not in a relationship, per se, he still wanted to know that she was safe.

He sat down at his desk and turned on the laptop. He pulled up his brief for the case he had coming up in Judge Richmond's court. He needed to be on his toes, with this one. There could be no room for error if he wanted to keep his perfect record. He looked over the evidence and read his client's statement several times. He needed to believe him, even if that belief was forced and unfounded. He rehearsed his closing statement, as was his custom.

Winter called, as he was citing his reasons for the jury to find his client not guilty.

"Hello, Winter," he greeted.

"I just wanted to let you know that I have made it home. Thank you for tonight, I needed that," she spoke softly into the phone.

"The pleasure was shared by the both of us," Jarhys assured.

They hung up from one another and Winter opened the car door. She walked up the stairs, from the garage and into the kitchen of the home that she shared with Gray Jenkins. She immediately knew something was amiss. She walked over to him and embraced him.

"What's going on, Gray," she asked as she ran her fingers through his hair. "You look like you've seen a ghost."

"Winter, it far worse than that, let me assure you."

She sat down at the kitchen table and listened with disbelief as Gray began to recant the scene he and Etmus had come upon by the river's edge. He wanted to erase it from his mind, but he feared it forever emblazoned there.

"I am sure you will find some solace during the service tomorrow, at church. Pastor Zeke always has a way of calming your spirit when things at work become overwhelming," Winter advised.

"I sure hope so. In the meantime, I am not sure I can sleep tonight."

"What about Etmus? How is he handling all of this?"

"He called his brother, Jackson, so they could meet up and have drinks. In fact, I could use one, myself."

"Let me get that for you, baby," Winter offered, as she rose from the chair and headed to the wet bar just outside of the kitchen. "What would you like?"

"Something strong," he called out.

"A scotch on the rocks it is," she replied.

CHAPTER NINE

The emergency room filled to capacity today. This was usual for the first weekend of the summer. Children were running wild and getting into trouble. College kids were home from the university and can be prone to excessive celebrating. However, today seemed out of the ordinary; there were more traumatic injuries coming in and requiring serious medical attention. Ziva Montgomery has seen two John Does come into the intensive care unit during the last week. Neither had identification and their faces were so distorted that they were going to be unrecognizable to loved ones. However, hospital staff took and sent pictures to the local police and other departments within a twenty-five mile radius of Mercy Medical Center in Dubuque, Iowa. Someone brought both men to the door of the ER, left them there until found by a passerby or medical staff.

Ziva prayed for the John Does as was her custom when anyone came to her floor. She made sure she walked to their rooms, closed the doors and walked the floor while waiting on

God to tell her what she should petition. It was the case with these men given to her charge as the clinical nurse leader in the intensive care unit. She requested ICU because it best fit with a gift that God had given her - the gift of healing. When she was at her post and patients came through, it was not long before they transitioned to the regular wards and then went home. To her dismay, neither man arrived while she was on the clock. Days had passed before she could check their chart and pay them a visit. She had been on vacation, tending to the needs of her husband and the church.

When she walked into the first man's room, that had arrived, she sensed heaviness in the room. She prayed and asked God to remove the weight, but it remained. Puzzled, she walked over to the bed to get a look at the young man. He was of medium build and height. His distorted and swollen face looked as if he had been a victim of an assault. He was in a coma and his vitals were weak and thread. The doctors in charge of his care were unsure of his prognosis. He remained unresponsive since the day he arrived and there seemed to be no remedy for the disfiguring inflammation of his face. As she began to pray, she heard the Lord say, "*It must be this way, for now, Ziva.*"

Her relationship with God was an intimate one. She knew His voice and she obeyed, not to say that she did not have questions. She wanted to know what was going on. She wanted God to give her a sense of peace about the situation that surrounded John Doe number one. Yet, He remained silent. She prayed about her impatience and her plaguing curiosity. She did not want to get in the way of God's work, so she needed to work on minding her business; and right now, that business was to trust God with this man. She needed to believe that the spiritual weight, in this room, would not affect the others on the ward. She walked out, knowing that God was in control of this young man's life and it was not her place to question Him.

Ziva walked into the room of the most recent arrival, the second John Doe. She was relieved when she did not encounter the same spiritual force, at work, in this room. However, there was something running amuck. She sensed a grating presence, one that irritated her. The air in this room felt oddly familiar, as if she had been in its company before. She prayed, in the

Spirit, for God to guard her heart and mind. She prayed for the surface of her skin, her eyes, her ears, her vocal cords and her limbs. She did not want any avenue of entry for this pervasive imp. She heard herself, quietly rebuking his presence and revoking its right to be in this room.

Mavet laughed at Ziva's attempt to evict him. He had every right to be in this room He was invited; he was like family. No matter how hard she prayed to her God, he was not going anywhere. He was not afraid of her. She should be afraid of him and the power he has; power that she does not understand. Nevertheless, he stayed in the corner, shrouded in the shadows. He watched her as she worked on the John Doe on the bed. He watched her examine his seriously jaundiced body. She peeked under his eyelids and checked his yellowed eyes. He knew this man had a life altering disease of the liver; the organ was necrotizing and nothing the doctors have done was working.

Ziva read the chart and a tear ran down her cheek. She asked God to spare his life because she sensed he had a family. He lay there, so still and yellow. This was one of the worst jaundice cases ever seen. His liver squeezed by its own death grip of dying tissue. He needed a new lease on life and she prayed he would get that opportunity. She wondered if he was a candidate for a liver transplant. She stared into his face hoping she could sense something about him that would help to notify his family. Someone should be here with him. She knew a loving presence when someone was this sick could make the world of difference. There have been miraculous events when someone who knew and loved a patient, someone who refused to remain silent, but speak to him or her in a way that would usher that person back into the land of the living.

As she turned to walk out of the door, she heard Mavet's raspy voice, *"The wages of sin is death."*

Doctor Nora Palmer sat in her office staring at the x-ray she had just received from the emergency room. She sighed. She became a pediatric cardiologist because she wanted to help sick children. This little boy was suffering from aortic regurgitation, a condition that allows blood to leak back into the heart because the valve does not close properly. His parents noticed that he was becoming increasingly more fatigued, from mild exercise. Once he began to complain about chest pain, they took him to his pediatrician who noticed a heart murmur. The doctor advised that murmurs were common in children, and if he continued to complain for them to return to him so that he could refer the child for a consult.

After a week had passed, with no further complaints of pain, the parents thought things were good and allowed the boy to return to normal activities. Today, while playing soccer, the young child passed out while running across the field. Rushed to Mercy Medical Center, the emergency room x-rays showed a significant aortic insufficiency. He is going to require valvuloplasty, surgery that will help create better function of the aortic valve, and lifelong follow up with a cardiologist.

Nora took a deep breath, to quiet the noise in her head. As much as she hated to admit it, Gavin's words caused her to pause. She had begun to question her abilities and had even turned down some very serious cases; referring them to her colleagues. She cited that she had a full plate and wanted the children to receive proper care from someone who had more time to dedicate to their case. In reality, she was afraid she would not be able to help them. She did not want to be the cause of a mother's pain. She knew that pain, all too well.

When she was a little girl, her mother found out that her sister had a heart condition. During that time, problems uncovered very late in the disease; and, little occurred to correct the issue. Her sister suffered several heart attacks before finally succumbing to endocarditis. Her mother's grief was all encompassing. Her father did everything he could to help his wife with the consuming guilt she felt because her child had died. Thank God for church and prayer. Her mother survived the ordeal, their family was intact and Katriel benefited as well. If it had not been for Nora's parents, she was not sure she would have been able to be the mother she is for her daughter, today. The fact that her parents had allowed them to move in with them while she finished her residency was a blessing.

Her mother survived one of the worst things a mother could endure. It was during her sister's illness that she vowed to become a pediatric cardiologist. She had always known she wanted to be a doctor; but watching the pain and suffering at the hands of such a tragic disease, she chose this field. It had been a rewarding field of choice, until Gavin poisoned it with his words. If truth were told, he was toxic to her confidence. She knew it was because he was not feeling good about himself, yet he had an amazing ability to twist his self-anger into a mighty weapon of destruction to those in his wake. He was wicked and she was weak. His incessant barrage of railing insults and vituperations have worn her down over the years. Nora could feel herself shrinking on the inside and she did not know what she could do about it. A final blow vanquished any fight she may have had. She was HIV positive. Her husband insured that she would be of no use to anyone, else. She could not leave him because who would have damaged merchandise.

He laughed when she told him. He told her it was her own fault. She probably obtained it while whoring around with the haughty doctors she worked with; he should be angry, he told her. He commenced to beating her for putting his life in danger. She could not go to work for days while the bruising and swelling were still evident on her face and arms. Nora could not even look Katriel in the face, during that time. She knew she was not setting the right example for her daughter. All she could do was pray to God to show her true love because she did not have the strength to be the mother her daughter needed. She was grateful for Pastor Zeke and First Lady Ziva for allowing Katriel to spend time with Marissa. She knew if she could see a healthy marital relationship that she would have a comparison to know that her family was not the norm. In fact, it was so broken that she was unsure why people could not see the cracks in the façade that she put on during church every Sunday.

She walked into church despondent and heartbroken, yet no one seemed to notice. Well, First Lady Ziva took notice and offered for her to come to the office to talk whenever she was ready. It was as she knew what was going on, but Gavin forbade her to burden the pastor's wife with her whining and ungratefulness. He told her that is why he brought her to church, so she could learn how to be appreciative of what she had and how good she had it. Plenty of women would love to be in her shoes, and she needed to understand that. In fact, he would flirt and carouse with the single women in the congregation while looking at her. He would point his hand at the women in a manner to say, 'You see this? I could have any one of them." She just put her head down and asked God to help her be more thankful.

Mavet approached her, one Sunday, asking her why she wanted to forgive her husband. He asked her if she ever wished him dead, so as to not have to endure the harshness of her reality. She had every right to be bitter and angry because of the lot she received. Why would God allow the pastor and his wife to have such a loving and caring relationship, while he sentenced her to a slow and painful self-death? Why would Gavin be so cordial and kind to other women and not to her, his own wife? She listened to him go on and on. She wanted to talk to someone about the pent-up frustrations with which she dealt. However, should she be talking to another man about her dissatisfaction in her marriage? First Lady approached her, while Mavet was still talking, and invited her to sit with her in the choir seats off to the side of the sanctuary. Nora wondered why she did not address Mavet, but shrugged it off, and followed her.

Nora shook her head to clear her thoughts. She needed to focus on the task. She had to tell this little boy's parents that he needed major heart surgery. She rose from her desk, grabbed the x-ray slides and headed out of her office.

Ziva Montgomery pondered on all of the puzzling spiritual warfare sourced through the hospital over the past week. She sought God and felt compelled to fast for Dubuque and Galena. She needed to pray for the children, the elderly and the hurting. She needed to pray for her husband, as the head of the Wisdom Outreach Center. She quieted her spirit to hear what God required of her through this time of meditation and consecration.

The alarm rang in the room for John Doe number two. The doctors hurried to his room and Ziva was on their heels, with the crash cart. He was experiencing an arrhythmia because his blood pressure was dropping. He looked agitated, as if he was in a fight. He struggled against the doctors and orderlies as they attempted to work on him to get his blood pressure under control. They pushed medication through his intravenous line. His whole body was in spasm. His arms flailed. His eyes fluttered, wildly, but they did not open. Then, the patient flat-lined, and the machine alarms were long and steady. The doctors pushed a twenty of epinephrine directly into the heart ... flat line. The doctor pulled the paddles from the defibrillator machine and called out, "Clear!" Electricity discharged through his heart due to the lethal arrhythmia. The heart monitor calmed down, as his heart returned to a normal sinus rhythm. His blood pressure rose slowly. The patient was out of the woods, for now, but remained in critical condition. Things were not looking good for John Doe; and he was all alone.

Ziva wondered why no one had reported this man missing. Was he a loner, walking through life with no one to care about him? A thought came to her, in that moment. She would not attribute it to God, but more of a remembrance. There was a man missing and presumed dead, in Galena. She believed his name was Maddock Hamilton. Could he be the missing man from her area? He is a member of the church, but she had not had an opportunity to get to know the young man. She stared into the yellowed face and willed herself to recognize him. Alas, it was a futile effort. She just did not have a good source to pull from to get a clear picture.

Mavet stood, as silent as he could, and watched the scene unfold before him. He did not want his friend to die; he owed him, too much.

As the doctors began to retreat out of the room, Ziva heard the rattling raspy voice, again. *The wages of sin is death*.

CHAPTER TEN

Babette Richmond hung up the phone. She was frustrated with the way this deal was panning out. This was supposed to be one of the easy ones, yet it was proving to be quite the opposite. With the man going missing in the Galena River Trails, the deal to sell the property just on the outskirts of the trail was beginning to unravel. The prospective buyers, a couple from Dubuque, were excited about their plans for the land along the Mississippi River's edge. Now, they were not so sure. The couple wanted to have a family and the development that was underway would have been the ideal start. However, with the violence now associated with the area, the clients were dropping like flies. The panic heightened because the man was still missing, and no suspect brought in for questioning.

She made several phone calls to the police department, requesting a consult with Chief Palmer, but had been unable to speak with him, directly. The department pushed her from officer to officer, each one unwilling to divulge any information on the case. She insisted that she needed some assurances or the development project would suffer a great financial loss, not excluding her and her firm. All she received was more stonewalling. She resorted to the damsel in distress role, which failed miserably. She moved to the angry citizen role, with the same fate. They were keeping the investigation and its status under wrap. Babette knew what that meant; they did not have a break in the case and did not want to alarm the community.

The real estate lawyer leaned her head back onto the camel-tone, leather office chair. She needed something to take her mind off of her professional woes. She closed her eyes and conjured up thoughts of her family. She pictured her loving husband, the circuit court judge, Honorable Cale Richmond. She adored him. He was her second spouse after marrying the wrong man, the day she graduated from college. Cale is the antithesis of her first husband, which is what drew her to him in the first place. She was not going to deny that James Walker was not a very good-looking man. Nor could she ignore the mind-blowing sex they shared. However, when she looked for solid reasons to remain in the relationship after she found him in his car with a prostitute, she could not find even one. All they shared, in common, was the sex. It was different with Cale.

Although the sex is more sedate, they were friends and that mattered to Babette. Cale was less attractive than James was, but he was sexy as hell in his black robe. He was intelligent and always willing to listen to her when she just wanted to talk. He did not attempt to fix every little thing that she complained about, either. He simply lent an ear or a shoulder and that was so important to her. When she needed him to step in and take control of the situation, he was always at the ready. He has never let her down in the nine years of their marriage. He was an amazing father, too. The kids loved him. He was as comfortable as a warm blanket on a cold Galena winter's night.

They got married almost immediately after starting to date. Her family and friends thought she was rushing into another relationship too soon after her annulment from James. She did not want to tell her family that she had a voracious sexual appetite and Cale matched her with frequency, if not intensity. She needed to marry Cale. She did not want to continue to have sex without being married, so they agreed that was the best move. What she did tell her family was that he was solid and dependable; she could tell that from the very beginning. On February 27, just three months after their first encounter, she became Mrs. Cale Richmond and she has not looked back since.

Babette does not regret the decision. They work well together, like a fine tuned machine, as her father would say. They were a team; Talia, Jonah and Brayden were blessed to have a good foundation from which to start their lives. They had parents that knew the value of togetherness and commitment. Sure, she had made a mistake by marrying James, but she did not repeat it in her marriage to Cale. She has no regrets and she prays that her husband does not either.

Although they both have high-pressure jobs, they find time for quality communication between the two of them and the children. Cale's schedule is fixed and stable. He is off on all major holidays, weekends and every evening. As a real estate lawyer, she has some flexibility for her evenings and weekends, as well. However, with this new development underway and the pressure to get things moving, she has been keeping some very late hours. She misses her husband and kids, but she is confident that they know she is doing this for them.

She has been battling the guilt that comes to every mother, or so she thinks, of having to leave her children in the hands of another to care for while she is at work. Her mother often said that it takes a village to raise a child. As grateful as she was for Sofia's willingness to add her children to her list of things to do every day, she can sense her disdain. Babette knows that Sofia is pro 'stay at home moms' and feels that every mother should make that sacrifice for the sake of their child. It works for her family, yet she should not judge other mothers for not making the same choice. Each family dynamic flows from different standards, choices and mandates. Their family's cohesiveness works because both she and Cale work. Her life is complete and she feels well rounded because she has the freedom to explore other things, as well as raise a family that knows they are loved.

The ringing of the telephone roused Babette from her reverie.

"Attorney Richmond, how may I help you," she answered.

It was a call from the rezoning committee at City Hall. The mayor's office needs more specs and architectural plans for the development. She assured the representative that the paperwork would be in their office by the close of business, today. Although she knew that the requested documents had been hand delivered to the office, weeks prior to today, she did not want to cause anyone to become disgruntled down at the hall. She needed everyone smiling and happy in her office, to keep the ball rolling in the right direction. Even with the hiccup of the missing person's case, Babette felt confident that the Galena Police Department would apprehend the culprit or locate the missing Maddock Hamilton. She did not care which one it was, just so long as it was one of them.

"Thank you for contacting me about it," she continued. "As I stated, I will personally ensure the papers get into your hands before four-thirty this afternoon."

After hanging up the phone, she walked over to the file cabinet in the furthest corner of her office and pulled out the drawer closest to the bottom. She reached into it, pulled out the requested papers and placed them into her briefcase. Babette grabbed her sunglasses off her desk, placed them on her face, and walked out of her office. This would give her an opportunity to see Cale, if his docket was clear; maybe he will have time to distract her from the delays her office is experiencing while waiting for some closure on this case.

The Galena Police Department was reeling with the news. When Etmus and Gray walked back into the squad room, they looked baffled and shaken. The captain approached them, requesting they go into an interrogation room to secure some privacy. He advised both men to go home after their encounter at the river's edge, a few days before. They called a back-up team to the scene, who took statements from the two officers. Neither of them was able to get any rest. At least Gray had Winter to go home to; Etmus went to an empty house after drinks with his brother, on that fateful day.

Captain Robert Powell closed the door behind Etmus, as he was the last to enter. He invited the men to sit down and asked them to recant the story, in his hearing.

"The chief followed us to the head of the trail where we mapped out a plan of who was going to do what at the scene. We stood in the parking lot talking amongst ourselves…well, we were talking while the chief was yelling," Gray corrected. His mind still clouded from the sight at the river and the lack of sleep.

"Once we were given our orders," Etmus picked up, "We began our trek into the forest area of the trail, while the chief returned to his car … car 50," he was beginning to lose focus.

"Settle down men," Robert urged. "We need a clear and concise recount of what took place on yesterday afternoon. Right now, we have a mess on our hands. We have a lot of questions and no solid, accountable answers."

"Gavin … I mean, the chief got into his car," Gray began again. "He sped off toward the US 20 Highway Bridge while we walked to the trail. We …my partner and I, decided it best if we split up in order to cover more ground in the least amount of time. We gave ourselves thirty minutes to meet back up at the path," his voice trailed off.

"That's when we heard it," Etmus stated.

"Heard what?" Robert questioned.

"That was when we heard the blood curdling scream coming from the direction of the river."

"We met back up, first," Etmus injected.

"Yes, we met back up, and then we heard the screams."

"Did you hear one scream or several screams?"

Gray and Etmus stared, blankly, at the captain.

"Did you hear one scream or several screams?" He asked, once more.

"Uh…" The two men looked at each other.

"Maybe it was several screams," Gray started.

"It could have been one long scream," Etmus added.

"We will come back to that part, continue," Robert encouraged.

"Well, we pulled our guns and rushed toward the sound of the screams … or scream,"

Gray's eyes darted wildly. Sweat began to bead upon his forehead.

"That's when we saw it … him," Etmus' voice trailed off.

"The birds were everywhere, flapping and squawking and flying around him … it."

"What the hell did you see?" Captain Robert Powell needed answers.

By the time the backup arrived on the scene, there was very little to find. They saw what they assumed was the Chief of Police, Gavin Palmer's revolver, on the ground, now with Ballistics for testing. The gun did not appear fired. Gavin's uniform was on the ground along with what appeared to be human organ in the mouth of a bird. The officers were able to retrieve pieces of it for examination. They did not want to jump to conclusions, but at this time, it appeared that they had a second missing person on their hands.

The department notified Gavin's family, but neither wife nor daughter had heard from him. They did not seem to be concerned about his absence, as it was his custom to go off for several days at a time. Robert had asked them to contact the department if they heard anything. However, until they made a statement to the police, there was nothing to report. However, he had a bad feeling, in his gut about this one. Yes, Gavin was prone to take off without a moment's notice from his family, but he was not one to miss consecutive days from work.

Robert had contacted Gavin's secretary and learned that Gavin had some vacation time. She offered that he could have taken some of it, as he had several weeks on the books. No one seemed to be concerned about the apparent disappearance of the chief of police. He looked at the two men, in front of them. He knew they saw something, but he was not getting anywhere with them, now. They were not going to be any good for anyone, in this condition.

"We are going to have the two of you go and talk to the department therapist. We need to get to the bottom of this," Robert said.

"Captain, what did the other officers see ..." the question fell off.

"The other officers retrieved a police revolver, from the ground and what appeared to be a human organ from a bird's mouth. There was some blood…"

"There was blood … a lot of blood," Gray interrupted.

"Yes, a lot of blood. But we cannot determine if it was human blood or the blood from the birds that had to be shot in order to get the organ out of their mouth."

The men looked ashen as he filled them in on the details.

"If you can tell me anything more …"

"Where's the chief, captain?" Gray asked.

"I was hoping the two of you could help me with that one."

They looked at each other, neither saying anything.

"Did either of you see Gavin, at the scene?"

"We don't know what we saw, Captain," both men spoke in unison.

"You saw the blood," Robert started.

"There was blood. There were birds and noise and ..."

"Birds and noise and what could have been a body, but ..."

"What do you mean, what could have been a body?"

"It had no substance or form, yet blood was pouring from somewhere."

"The birds were pecking it and the arms flailed at them trying to get them off of him ... or it."

"Captain, did the other officers see when they arrived?" The question echoed, again.

"I have already told you."

"Was it the chief?" Etmus asked.

Robert looked at the officers and felt a pang of sorrow for them. Whatever they saw has left an indelible impression on their psyche. They could not make sense of it. Their minds could not wrap around the scene as it unfolded in front of them. As it was, the backup officers shook at the thought that Gavin could be missing or worse, dead.

There was a knock on the interrogation room door, bringing a halt to the conversation. Robert rose from his chair and opened the door. There was a hushed conversation outside of the room. Etmus and Gray sat very still in their chairs, each one in his own private hell. They wanted to know what was going on. They wanted to know if that was the chief or something else, lying in the clutches of those voracious birds. What produced that scream that still echoes in their ears? And, what or who was lurking just behind the birds in the river with chains in its hands? Why do they think they heard the wind calling the chief's name?

Robert walked back into the room, closing the door behind him.

"We have a tentative report, from the tests. The organ that the birds were eating is human," He started.

"What was it?" Gray posed the question.

"A liver," Robert answered.

CHAPTER ELEVEN

Analise could not contain her glee. Her wedding day was just a couple of days away. The rehearsal dinner was to be held on tomorrow and her bridesmaids would be coming back to the house, with her to spend the night. Miles would be staying with his best man, Jarhys Houston, at his home along with the other groomsman, Jackson Harris. The guys have a bachelor party planned and the girls will be celebrating, as well.

Today, Mitrice and her crew would be at Turner Hall preparing it for the rehearsal dinner, as well as the wedding and reception. Her parents would be arriving this afternoon, and Miles' parents will be coming in early tomorrow. Both sets of parents had moved out of Galena, now excited to be returning to see their long-time friends. The Fitzhughs would pick up her parents and take them to a hotel. She would meet them there, however, there was too much to do to deal with her parents, tonight. Thank God, the Fitzhughs would be entertaining them and catching up on old times. Adley and Maren Dane volunteered to chauffer Miles' parents from the airport. The Kirkpatricks were excited to be coming home for their son's wedding and to see their friends, the Danes. It was all falling into place.

Analise was talking to Ghrelin, while she got dressed for the day. Their conversation started with patting herself on the back for having such foresight in purchasing the shawl for her dress. The local weather forecaster stated it will be sunny and clear Thursday, Friday, Saturday, and Sunday; a cool start to the summer of 2011, he added. The average temperatures, this time of year is normally in the lower eighties. This is why she chose the strapless Mia Solano original gown in diamond white. The dress is exquisite. The mermaid style, taffeta and lace dress wrapped around her figure, beautifully. Miles was going to go insane watching her sway her hips down the aisle toward him. This week, however, they ranged from the mid-sixties to lower seventies throughout the weekend, excluding Sunday, which would be in the upper seventies.

Ghrelin advised that she should not pout over the weather, she was about to live out her dream wedding. She was going to have it all; the expensive gown, the best hall with the theatrical lighting, expensive flowers, wine and food. She was going to be the belle of the ball as all eyes would be on her, as she glided on silk rose petals in her Dolce and Gabbana high shine, calf leather, peep toe courts. He congratulated her on the choice to have no veil because this would allow everyone to see her gorgeous face as she made her way toward her groom. Not to mention the fact that she chose a simple strapless Mia Solano, in mango, for her bridal party; this would ensure that no one would steal the show.

Analise smiled at the genius. She has some beautiful friends, with great bodies. She could not put them in a dress that would draw attention to them and take the focus off her. Winter and Alaina were successful, in their fields, which added to their appeal. Therefore, she decided to tone down their attraction by putting them in a simple, yet elegant dress. She was grateful that both women sported short dos and she insisted that their makeup be modest for the occasion. They would be carrying a simple long-stemmed orchid. She knows people are going to be surprised that there are only two women, in her bridal party, with her reputation for 'more.' However, it was unimaginable that someone would not take the spotlight off her, with a large group of women. Consequently, she chose the two women who were the most secure and understanding of her personality.

Winter Pharron is one of her longest standing friends. They met in college and almost immediately, they became acquainted. Analise had her moments of jealousy, when it came to her friend, but she was able to keep it concealed most of the time. Winter had a way with men that baffled Analise. She could attract any man of her choosing, no matter their race, creed or pedigree. Most African American females at the college snubbed their nose at her, but not Analise. She envied her and wanted to have what she possessed.

Ghrelin would tell her to study Winter like she was one of her subjects. He encouraged her to take mental notes of the things she admired most and commit them to memory. Analise would try to emulate the undercurrent of what she thought her friend was doing, but she would make it her own. There was no way she would have another woman saying that she was a carbon copy of her. She wanted to be original and have her own flair. She still seemed to come up short, whenever the two of them were together. Thus, she resorted to using her body to steer the men away from Winter. The competitiveness of their relationship was one-sided, however. Her friend never volleyed for the attention of men, or anyone else, for that matter.

Alaina Toussaint, a fellow teacher at Galena High School, and Analise had been friends for years. She taught French to the seniors who were looking to transition to careers that required them to be fluently bilingual. She did not want the kids who were just taking a language to fulfill the graduation mandate; she wanted those who were serious enough to move into fields that would suit their skill level. She was born on the French isle of Corsica, where her family business was in gastronomy, the pleasures of fine dining and good wine. When asked why she would leave one of the most beautiful islands in the Mediterranean Sea, to come to Illinois, she simply replied … *"Love, of course."*

Ghrelin and Analise shook themselves from their reverie in order to get their day started. Miles was at work and she was going to meet the girls for lunch before heading over to get their dresses. She dressed, grabbed her purse and they headed out of the door.

Winter arrived at I Do Bridal, LLC ahead of Analise and Alaina. She found a parking space on North Commerce Street and walked into the shop. The sales representative greeted her and asked if she was with a party. She confirmed that two other women would be meeting here for the final fitting and pickup of their dresses. She sat, in the waiting area, perusing magazines. She reached for a bottle of water from a tray that was sitting off to the side and opened it. Before she could take a sip, Analise and Alaina walked into the shop.

"I will never understand why you rush off when we are headed in the same direction." Analise stated.

"Don't judge me, my friend. I will drive as I see fit. Besides, you do not have to understand me." Winter winked.

"There, there, girls – put those claws away." Alaina teased.

The saleswoman walked over to the three women and guided them to the fitting rooms. Each woman was directed to try on the dresses and come out into the common area to view them. Winter headed for room number two, Analise walked into room number one, leaving Alaina room number three. Just before stepping over the threshold, she glanced over as Winter went into her assigned room. She smiled.

Alaina found it difficult to concentrate, as she began to disrobe. Her mind filled with visions and her olfactory center rushed with a distracting fragrance. She could hear Winter as she removed her clothing and hung them on the wall hook. She listened as Analise asked the sales representative to assist her with tying the bodice and she was still fully clothed. She hurried to catch up with the other two women, so they would be in the common area, together.

When the two women came out and saw Analise in her dress, they were astonished at her beauty. The diamond white dress was an amazing contrast to her cocoa brown skin. The bodice wrapped around her breast, while taffeta ribbon crisscrossed at her small waist.

The lace embroidery encircled her hips and dipped down the center of her buttocks trailing down her legs, ending at the taffeta bow just behind her knees. Taffeta pleats flowed out, mermaid style onto the floor covering her feet.

"You look amazing!" Winter exclaimed.

"Analise, you will have Miles drooling as you walk down the aisle." Alaina added.

Ghrelin agreed with both women, as he stared in admiration at his long-time friend. He was content just being a part of this special moment with Analise. He encouraged her to drink it all in and allow herself to digest every minute of it. She would need room for more, as her wedding day approached. She reveled in the atmosphere of approbation, the enthusiastic express of approval from her friends and confidante. Tears welled up in her eyes, as they lavished compliments upon her. She wanted more. She hugged herself and twirled around like a teenage girl. Ghrelin smiled.

Winter was smiling at her friend and was feeling genuine happiness for her, in this moment. She knew she had been reaching for this very moment, since college. Analise wanted to be the lone star in a man's galaxy, thus gaining his approval through gifts. There was no disputing that her love language was gift giving. She felt most loved when plied with presents and all manner of dainties. Thank goodness, Miles knew his bride-to-be and was at peace with her capaciousness.

Winter looked over in the direction of Alaina and noticed she had been looking at her. They smiled at one another; each knowing that their friend was relishing in the attention. The salesperson called her associate over to look at one of the most beautiful brides they have had the pleasure of outfitting. Another woman came into the shop, complimented Analise on her choice, and wished her well.

After a small alteration to Alaina's dress, the three friends walked out of the store with their bridal ensemble in tow. Each carefully placed her dress on the backseat of their car before heading to the respective destinations.

Analise felt so good after picking up her dress that she wanted share her good mood with her fiancé. She decided she would take the twenty-five minute ride from Galena to Hanover and surprise Miles in his office. She hopped onto

US Highway 20/Illinois 84 and turned on the CD player, in her car. The miles melted away, as she sang her favorite songs, and before long she was turning right onto Commercial Drive.

After finding a parking space and putting her dress in the trunk of her car, Analise walked into the office building. She smiled and greeted the security guard and lobby desk attendant, then headed toward Suite One. She opened the door, closed it behind her and sauntered to the desk at her smiling man.

"Baby, what a surprise," Miles whispered, as he covered the receiver of the phone.

"I just had to see you," Analise whispered back, as she straddled him in his black leather office chair.

She wrapped her arms around his neck and kissed him on the opposite side of where he was holding the phone. She let her tongue trace a path from his ear to his collarbone, then back again.

"Something has come up. Can I call you back, in a few?" Miles questioned. He hung up the phone and welcomed Analise's mouth with his own.

"Something has come up," she stated as she rubbed her hips into his groin.

"I thought you wanted to wait until our wedding night before we made love, again," Miles stated. He caressed her legs as he moved toward her generous bottom.

"I do…" she started. "At least, I thought I did," she finished.

His hand traveled up her waist and cupped her breasts. He lifted the dress up and over her outstretched arms. His fingers tickled her sides, then the lower part of her back. He reached up to unfasten the clasps on her bra. An impassioned sigh escaped his lips as her breasts freed and she arched herself backward to ensure easy access to her nipples. He flicked one with his tongue, then the other. He could feel the warmth emanating from her private area, as she moved her hips and sighed.

"I just picked up my wedding dress," she moaned as his hands reached inside her panties.

The ride home, from Miles' office was a good one. Analise felt good, inside and out. She was really a lucky woman. She was certain there were few females who could boast of a successful, good-looking man, let alone one who could satisfy her every need. He did not pull any punches when it came to making sure she was happy and well taken care of, in all aspects of their relationship. He catered to her every whim and he was not afraid to sample new things. She needed a man like Miles Kirkpatrick and she was delighted to have found him.

As she pulled into the driveway of the home she shared with her soon to be husband, Ghrelin stood waiting. He could sense her good mood before she got out of the car. She pushed the button, on the keyless remote to open the trunk of her car. She reached in, grabbed her dress before closing it back and heading toward the stairs and her dearest compatriot. He reached for her and they walked into the house, arm in arm.

"I see that Miles has done it again," Ghrelin stated.

"Doesn't he always, Ghrelin? I mean there has never been a time that I have not come away with everything," she smiled, "Pun intended."

Ghrelin grew quiet.

"You are not jealous, my dearest, are you?" Analise asked.

"I have no reason to be, my sweet. We have shared more intimate moments, than you and your love Miles has, over the years."

"Indeed, we have," Analise agreed.

"I do not have to enter you, to be a part of you. I am quite satisfied knowing your deepest secrets."

"Good," Analise said. "I am quite satisfied with you knowing them."

The two friends walked into the living room. Ghrelin took a seat, while Analise went into the kitchen to get something for them to drink. She sat next to him and sighed.

"Life is good."

"It can only get better," Ghrelin asserted.

"And that it will. In just a couple of days, I will become Mrs. Miles Kirkpatrick and everyone will witness it."

"You will be doing it up, in style, too. Walking toward your man, in an exquisite gown, fabulous shoes, expensive flowers and theatrical lighting – you will be the envy of every bride in Galena."

"I will, won't I?"

"Yes, you will."

The two of them fell silent as they explored their own thoughts. They sat back and put their feet up on the coffee table. All the while Mavet was standing in the corner, unnoticed by either of them.

CHAPTER TWELVE

Cale Richmond loved his job. He had fought hard as an attorney to get here. He did not let anything get in his way. He cleared his plate, at home and at work, in order to focus on the undertaking – becoming the first African American Circuit Court Judge in Jo Daviess County. He had higher aspirations, but he would temper those until his children were older. They deserved to have a chance at a stable childhood before he started moving them around as he volleyed for a position in the Supreme Court. His beautiful wife also deserved a shot at the limelight in her field. There is a big development in the works and she will have played a big role in making it happen. He loved his wife and his family. They were one of the most important things, in his life. He enjoyed his life and he put it all on the table to make sure that it stayed that way.

He went hard after everything he wanted. He left nothing to chance because it had a way of backfiring on a person. He takes life by the horns and rides it for all it is worth. He has been this way his entire life. His mother and father always said he had a lust for life. His mother went into premature labor, while pregnant with him. The doctors did not expect him to live being born two months early. Yet, he fought like a soldier and held on. He was breathing on his own and eating with gusto well ahead of the skeptical timetable set by the specialists. He refused to let their word be the last word, his father had told him.

Cale was the same, today. There was nothing allowed to stand in the way of his dreams or goals. He did not let anything stop him from going after what he wanted. There were no vows, laws or covenants to impede his progress toward his desired end. He did not deem it untoward indulging himself, from time to time with the pretty, little aids that dusted the courtroom floor. They were eager and power hungry, which led to him getting his appetite sated at his disposal. Today was no exception.

This young paralegal, in his office now, was handling his most pressing needs. As her head bobbed up and down on his erect penis, he sat back in the judge's chambers looking around at the décor. She was not as talented as others had been, or his wife for that matter. She was, however, eager to please and that had to count for something. When he felt himself growing soft, he had to conjure up thoughts of this wife's beautiful breasts. They never failed to get a rise out of him. He smiled as he hardened in her mouth. He kept the picture in his mind until he was fully satisfied.

The paralegal wiped her mouth and stepped away from his desk. "Is there anything else I can do for you, Your Honor?" she asked as she straightened her clothes and smiled.

"No, sweetheart, you have done well," he lied. He was bored and not engaged as she performed fellatio on him.

"Well, then, I will leave this deposition on your desk and be on my way," she looked like she was waiting for something.

He sure did hope she was not expecting him to return the favor. She did not perform as if she wanted anything; it was quite lackluster. Some came in her giving it their all, thus causing him to want to repay their efforts. This was no such attempt.

"Thank you, umm,"

"Candace," she stated a bit forlornly.

"Thank you, Candace."

He took a file from his drawer and turned his chair around to face the window, his way of dismissing those who would not leave on their own. He had several cases on his docket, today. He enjoyed Thursdays in the summer because it was the start of his weekend. Jo Daviess closed the courthouse on Fridays from mid-June to early September. This week, Cale had plans with the kids and his wife. He was looking forward to their trip to Palace Campgrounds where he has a reserved cabin for his family. The goal is to leave, tonight, after he gets off and return in time for church at the Wisdom Outreach Center on Sunday.

He looked at the clock on the wall and realized it was time for him to take the bench for the afternoon court session. He checked the docket and realized there was a continuance request for the last hearing for today. He was pleased about it until he recognized the name of the lawyer scheduled to try the case, Winter Pharron. He could feel himself getting aroused just thinking about the lawyer. She was beautiful to look at, yet her fragrance drove him mad as he listened to her make her case. On several occasions, he was glad to have on the long robe and be sitting behind such a large desk. He was disappointed that he would not get an opportunity to breathe her in, this afternoon.

"Oh well, there is always next week," he said, aloud, as he rose to take his place.

As he opened the doors leading from his chambers to the bench, he heard the bailiff speaking.

"All rise for the Honorable Cale Richmond."

Everyone stood until he sat and spoke.

"You may be seated," Cale stated. He noticed Mavet sitting in the back of the courtroom. There was an imperceptible nod of greeting between the two as he advised the court clerk to call the first case.

Sofia Koen knew today was going to be a short one because the Richmonds were going out of town with their children. She had been thinking about the trip and wondering why they would be spending their money taking the children camping when they could be saving it for something more, like their college fund. She never understood how people were so dull when it came to setting their priorities in order. There were plenty of day trips that would be just as enjoyable; and, there was extra money to save and use toward something more long-lasting and beneficial.

Mavet inserted the fact that not everyone had what it took to make the sacrifices that she had made for her family. She took special care to secure the future of her children and the welfare of her family.

"Some people spend without thinking. Just because they have jobs, right now, doesn't mean that things could not change. Babette should be thinking about her children. Cale should be thinking about his family. Instead they are wasting money on camping trips."

"They are being irresponsible," Mavet added.

"To say the least!" she finished.

"African Americans are always looking for ways to spend and not save," Mavet incited.

"Well, it is across the board, Mavet. It is not just African Americans, there are plenty of

Caucasians and other races that choose the route of spend more," she did not take the bait.

"But haven't you noticed that the black people that you know have very little savings and are always looking to make a new purchase," he would not let up.

"Well, yes … but, I have some Jewish friends who are doing the same thing. They think the money will always be there."

"But people of color are always looking to keep up with the Jones', so to speak. They insist on getting every new thing, going to the newest places to eat," he continued.

"Mavet, what is going on?" Sofia turned to him with an inquisitive look on her face. "You are sounding like you are a racist."

"I am not a respecter of persons, Sofia. I am merely making an observation."

"Well, I have noticed this with several people of all races. They make purchases better left unmade. They take trips that deplete their account, unnecessarily. Levi and I are not like that. I am not saying that we do not want the finer things, in life, because we do. What I am saying is that moderation is the key."

"Cale could be using that money toward expanding his house to increase the equity," Mavet stated.

"That is exactly what I am talking about, Mavet. They should not be spending time and money on a camping trip that the kids will not remember. It will not benefit them, unless they plan to teach them something. However, I doubt that. They are probably too tired to do anything constructive with them, especially with it just being for the weekend."

Mavet nodded his head in agreement and they sipped on brewed iced tea. Sofia liked to consider herself as the perfect homemaker. Her ideation was simple, take care of your family and your family will take care of you. She made her children's juice from produce bought from the farmer's market. She did not agree with those mothers who served their children soft drinks and processed juice. Her meals were well thought out and purchased organically, when possible. She knew what it took to take care of what she needed to and she did it. Being self-sufficient is the only way to do anything. She understood the need to be able to do everything herself, just in case she was on her own. Her ability to trust what she cherished most into the hands of anyone else was taboo. *I can do it, myself, and often have to*, was her silent mantra.

"Babette should have taken it upon herself to insist that this trip not be made a priority. Sometimes it is the job of the wife to step in and be the voice of reason. Men, no offense Mavet, occasionally need a nudge in the right direction."

She often thought about the sermons she heard over the pulpit that directed the parishioner to trust God with their lives. What a bunch of hogwash! Sure, she believed that God created the earth and that His Son took the blame for most of what humans get into, but what did that have to do with the everyday living of life? God was not going to, mysteriously, put money in someone's bank account; that person had to earn it. He was not going to, magically, place knowledge in someone's head; that person had to educate him or herself. The onus is on the individual to make things happen, if it was going to happen at all. Too often, the Christian sits back as if the finer things in life are going to fall into their laps. Alternatively, they believe that things will get better without blood, sweat and tears – she believed people had to roll up their sleeves and get the job done, on their own. God was not some genie in a lamp waiting to do the bidding of any passerby. Things are done and blessings are wrought, at the hand of those who work toward it.

Sofia was often disappointed in those people who stood up in the church and lied about God doing something without man's effort. Those who believed stories saddened her - fables of bills paid, homes obtained, and other material gain came with no effort on their part. She hated when she heard the catty women talking about, "when the praises go up, the blessings come down." She wanted to scream. When your husband took his behind to work, you were able to pay your bills and buy some groceries. She believes God adds His hand to the efforts of man. True godliness displays by the hard work put forth by those who choose to believe in His goodness. Humankind makes God look good by giving Him the credit for the work of their own hands.

Sofia understood that many people would not come right out and say it the way she felt it should be said. She knows that instead they will say they are trusting God, when behind the scenes they are devising plans to certify their outcome is what is seen. She knows that people will say that God paid a bill, when in fact it was the wife calling on others to assist in their time of need. How many wives or husbands believe that their spouse is putting their heads in the sand, when there are pressing matters in their homes? They say they are praying – hoping and believing that by some divine work of providence something will come through for them. Then say it was God when in fact, it was overtime put in or a second job obtained to bring the money in.

"Mavet, I sure do hope that Cale isn't using bill money to take this trip. I would hate for Babette to have to pick up the slack because her husband insists on being able to tell his friends that he is doing something."

"Well, maybe they believe that God will provide for them," Mavet added.

"God bless the child that has his own, is my motto."

Moments later the winds picked up and the tree limbs bent under the pressure. Dust and debris was coming in from the wooded area behind the house and it was becoming difficult for Sofia to see the kids. It sounded like she heard Levi's car pulling up in the driveway, but she wanted to insure that the children were safe before heading in to greet him. She got up from her seat and walked farther into the backyard. She called for the kids to answer, but the wind was howling. She could not remember whether they were calling for storms. Perhaps, this was some freak tempest that popped up unexpectedly. She attempted to shield her face from the swirling dirt, but was unsuccessful. Her eyes, ears and mouth had been infiltrated.

Sofia called for the children, again. She did not realize how far she had gone into the yard until she thought she could make out the impression of the trees, in the near distance. She put a forearm over her eyes and squinted, trying to see if she could focus to see the children. As she strained to see, she sensed a presence very close to her. She turned abruptly, but no one was there. The wind was so loud and she was beginning to think the children would have run into the house, with all of this commotion.

She began to turn back, but was suddenly whipped about by what she thought was a gust of wind. She felt a hand grab her left arm and a stabbing fear gripped her heart. She strained to see and became ashen as she saw yellow eyes staring back at her. A sharp pain pierced her left side just before the darkness fell.

Levi could not understand the tumult that seemed to be coming from his backyard. When he came into the house, the children who had come inside greeted him. He walked toward the patio doors that opened up to the back of the house and quickly turned back in horror. He ushered the children out of the room and insisted they go up into the playroom on the second floor. There was no way he was going to allow them to see what he just saw.

CHAPTER THIRTEEN

Mitrice procured the airline tickets and hotel reservations for the Mitchells and the Kirkpatricks. The Ramada Inn had given her a good rate for both sets of parents and the other guests that were flying in from various parts of the country. This was also the site of the wedding day's activities for the women in the group. Mrs. Mitchell, Mrs. Kirkpatrick, Analise, Winter and Alaina were to spend most of the day in the spa, located inside of the hotel. Indulge Day Spa was booked months before this day and they were ready for the bridal party when they arrived for the Day of Bliss Spa Package. Each woman was to receive a fifty minute Bliss massage, a radiant facial, a grand manicure and pedicure, hair and make-up to prepare them for the wedding this evening. The spa manager was gracious enough to include Mitrice au gratis. Of course, she would not be with the wedding party, but she would be lavished with some much needed pampering.

This wedding has proven to be one of her more difficult assignments. Analise Mitchell was not the easiest person to accommodate. She was never satisfied, always wanting more. Every time she thought she had gotten her to a good place, accepting of the plans, she would ask for something else. Mitrice could not understand her need for excess, but she wasn't being paid to understand. Boy, had she heard that enough during her tenure as wedding planner for Analise.

There was one shining light, which could make this whole experience worthwhile for Mitrice - Jackson Harris, the groomsman in the wedding party. She met him, for the first time, last night and she was smitten. She knew she was too old for a schoolchild's crush, but this is what it felt like. He was so cooperative at the rehearsal, which helped a great deal because all of them seemed a bit off their game. This was a small wedding party, with one maid of honor, a best man, a bridesmaid and a groomsman. She wondered if they had been out drinking prior to coming to the rehearsal because the women were giggling and falling out of sync with the men while walking. She thought this was a bit disrespectful with Pastor Montgomery in attendance. On the other hand, again, this was not her concern. She finally got them together and tried to gain some confidence that they would remember all of this when it really counted.

Jackson was not like that, at all. He seemed to take things more seriously than even the bride did. This surprised Mitrice, especially the way Analise had carried the planning phase of her big day. She was nonchalant and was more concerned about merrymaking than assuring everyone knew his or her places for the ceremony. Pastor Montgomery did not seem to be bothered by their shenanigans and for that, she was grateful. It was rare to see a minister assume a nonjudgmental air in the face of some blatant disrespect. However, Jackson stood out amongst the others, not to say that any of the men were out of line. In fact, they handled the women's giddiness in stride. She noticed that the best man seemed to know just what to say to the bridesmaid to get her to settle down. They 'felt' very familiar to Mitrice; although she was certain that Winter was in a relationship with another man. Not that it mattered to most people, these days.

Before leaving, Jackson asked her for her number and stated he would like to go out and get to know her better. He knew now was not the time, but instead it would be ideal after the wedding when her assignment was finished. It took her off guard to hear him refer to her job as an assignment; that is how she approached each job. His astuteness stood out and was an instant attraction for her. She could not get him off her mind. She talked to the Lord about him, on the ride home from the rehearsal and rehearsal dinner. She found herself praying for him before she went to sleep, last night. Now, she was daydreaming about their date. A date that had no timetable or definite form, yet she planned her outfit and wondered what they would talk about. She knew he was a firefighter and that made him even more intriguing. He chose a profession that would put his life in danger, in order to save others. She berated herself for romanticizing about his profession. It seemed so adolescent.

The appointment for the Day of Bliss Spa Package was set for ten o'clock this morning, to conclude at two o'clock this afternoon. This would allow them time to go into the bridal suite, already reserved for the couple to spend the night before heading to the airport in the morning, and prepare for the wedding. The carriage was reserved between the hours of four and eight o'clock this evening. Jack's Galena Carriage Company will be transporting the bride to Turner Hall for the wedding and then the couple to Grant Park for pictures at the pavilion, gazebo, fountain, trellis and bridge. Afterward, they would return to Turner Hall and join the guests at the reception. Mitrice contacted the photographer from Elite Images and the videographer from Sight and Sound Productions to confirm they would be in place at the appropriate time. Everyone was good to go, enabling her to breathe a big sigh of relief.

Mitrice wondered what kind of mischief everyone got into last night. She overheard Jarhys Houston arranging for strippers to come to his house, last night after the rehearsal dinner. She, also, knew that Winter procured male strippers for Analise's final night as a single woman. Mitrice could not help but wonder if Jackson enjoyed watching strange women flaunt their naked bodies in front of him. She shook her head, at her foolishness. What man would not enjoy a woman's naked body? A gay man, she mused.

The women gathered in the lobby of the Ramada Inn at nine forty-five looking tired and worn. Mitrice never understood the fun in burning the midnight oil when there was such a big day ahead. *No judging, Mitrice*, she reminded herself. Not everyone was going to handle things the way she did and it was not her place to put expectations on others based on her own assumptions and values. She put on her most professional smile and greeted each woman, cordially. She arranged for one of the associates from the Indulge Day Spa to meet them in the lobby to escort the party to the facility. The woman was prompt.

"Good morning, ladies," she greeted. "My name is Marilyn and I will be your attendant throughout your experience at Indulge Day Spa."

Each woman said their hellos as they followed Marilyn through the lobby and down the corridor. Once they got to the end of the hall, she opened the doors and stepped aside allowing each woman to walk into the spa. Once everyone transitioned into the capable hands of the staff, the attendant turned to Mitrice.

"Right this way," she directed her through another door and down a luxurious corridor.

Garden Party Florists had outdone themselves with this wedding party. The hall was astonishing with the arrangements of rainbow roses and scattered petals along the aisle where the bride was to traverse to meet her groom. The silk imitations were so realistic that Mitrice bent down to insure they were not the real thing. There was no way she could have rainbow roses bleeding onto Analise's white gown as she walked down the aisle. To top it all off, it smelled amazing in hall. The scent of roses and orchids danced in the atmosphere and tickled the nose in the most pleasing manner. She was certain the bride would be happy with this. She smiled.

She stood at the doorway to await the bridal party's arrival to the hall. The men were the first to pull up. Mitrice tried to remain as professional as she could when she saw Jackson step out of the limousine in his cream-colored tuxedo with a cummerbund and bowtie to match the mango color of the bridesmaid dress. He smiled at her and touched her hand before heading to their assigned room. Taken aback at his forward gesture, the touch seemed more intimate than it should have been and she wondered what type of woman he thought she was. She would not allow herself to become crestfallen about something that she was unsure of, so she tabled it until she could ask him what he meant by it.

The limousine with Alaina and Winter arrived, shortly thereafter. The driver opened the door for the women and escorted them up the stairs to where Mitrice was standing, waiting for them.

"As soon as the carriage arrives with Analise, we will head to the room assigned for the bridal party," Mitrice advised.

Moments later, Jack's Galena Carriage Company was turning the corner. The videographer and photographer jumped out of their cars, leaving them unmanned in the middle of the street, in order to catch this moment for posterity. Analise had the shawl wrapped around her shoulders, but it did not take away from the stunning beauty of her gown. Passersby stood and applauded as the horse-drawn carriage made its way toward the favored venue for wedding events in Galena. She glowed under the attention of mere strangers and Mitrice felt a prick in her heart at the sight. She could feel the longing, in this woman's heart, as she craved the attention.

She wanted it and more. She seemed insatiable in her need to obtain things, anything, whether it was material items or notice of everyone around her.

The carriage stopped, the driver hopped down and retrieved the stepping stool used to assist the passengers to and from the buggy. He placed it on the ground and reached his hand up to Analise. Her gloved hand held onto his as he helped her down and guided her to the sidewalk. The limousine transporting the parents of the bride and groom pulled up behind the carriage. Analise's father held onto his wife with one hand and reached for his daughter with the other. He led both women up the stairs of Turner Hall and into the lobby area.

Mitrice signaled the musicians to begin to play soft music while the ushers walked the mothers into the hall to take them to their seats. Miles' father walked behind the women and took the seat next to his wife, while Mr. Mitchell walked with his daughter to the room where Alaina and Winter were waiting. Mitrice went to the men's room and softly knocked on the door.

"It is time to take your place Miles," she spoke, as the door opened.

"You ready, man?" Jarhys asked.

"As ready as I'll ever be," Miles answered. He swiped at a stray blond hair.

"I told you to consider getting a haircut," Jackson stated.

"She loves my hair this way. She loves to run her fingers through it when we..." he winked and they all laughed.

"T.M.I., dude. Keep that to yourself," Jackson chuckled.

Mitrice motioned for Miles to take his place off to the side of Pastor Montgomery. She noticed his cheeks were getting red, which was a telltale sign of his nervousness. She hoped enthusiasm took its place when he saw how spectacular his bride looked as she walked down the aisle to meet him. She took note of the pastor patting him on the shoulder and whispering something in his ear. The redness dissipated and a genuine smile of expectancy adorned his face. She walked back to the rooms where the men and women were waiting. She directed them to stand in the hallway, just as they had practiced. She caught a quick glimpse of Jarhys eyeing Winter with the slightest glimmer of desire; she returned the look.

Alaina paired with Jarhys, as she was the maid of honor. Jackson took Winter's arm and wrapped it loosely around his. Mitrice had to admit this was a very handsome wedding party. Analise was arm in arm with her father, who had been wiping tears from his eyes. She leaned into his shoulder and looked up into his face. The photographer trained to capture moments like this, and he was right there snapping a picture of the touching moment. The videographer was positioned in the front of the hall awaiting the march of the bridal party.

Mitrice signaled the musicians, again and the soloist began to sing while Jackson and Winter began their walk down the aisle. In step and several bars later, Jarhys and Alaina made their way to their appointed positions. She found herself watching Jackson's long legs walking in time to the music. He was good eye candy and she hoped he thought of her as good to look at, as well.

The soloist finished the song and took his seat. Pastor Montgomery waited for Mitrice's signal, then asked the attendees to please stand and the wedding march began to play. The photographer had stepped inside the hall and hurried to the front to get the perfect shots of the bride walking down the aisle. Garden Party Florist had someone on site to refresh the silk petals prior to the bride descent to meet her groom.

Everyone turned to face the entryway as Analise and her father headed to the front of the church. His eyes brimmed with tears that he willed to not to fall. She, on the other hand, let her tears flow freely. The make-up artist assured that her make-up was waterproof and would withstand tears. She knew her entrance would be dramatic with the theatrical lighting dancing all around her as she walked. She could hear the clicking of cameras and her eyes glistened as the flashes lit up the room. The mango and white Ecuadorian roses in her bouquet beautifully contrasted the diamond-white gown. She felt like a princess and her father was the king. Her smile was unmatched as she saw the look in her groom's eyes as he watched her walking toward him. She wanted to remember that look for the rest of her life.

He could not hide his desire for her and she wanted to fan the flames.

Ghrelin sat mesmerized in his seat as he watched his friend walking down the aisle. She was everything she wanted to be, in this moment, and more. He smiled because he knew how happy she would be with the *more* part. Ever since she was a little girl, this exact scene was growing within her. She wanted to appear larger than anyone she had ever known. Right now, at this exact time, she was where she wanted to be - at the center of everyone's universe. All eyes were on her and it could not have been more glorious. He could feel the pull within her. She wanted this moment to last forever. She thought about what she could have done to make this second bigger and better.

Ghrelin began to worry. He sensed her desire grow to its largest heights deep within her belly. With each step, she was regretting the last and hoping for more on the next. Her tears were no longer of joy but of fear. She did not want this to end. She wanted, no needed, more attention. He noticed Mavet standing across the aisle from him. He looked as if he would grab her right out of the hands of her father, but he stood his ground. Everyone wanted her, or so she told herself. A whirlwind of emotions spiraled within her. Memories from times past, those she thought she had wished away, swept back into the forefront. Her feelings of inadequacy, her fears of not being enough and her need to fill her emptiness were swirling around in her belly.

Analise doubled over, grabbed her midsection and let out one of the most tormented screams those in attendance had ever heard. The room went black, as Evan Mitchell reached for his daughter. When the lights came back on, everyone in the room began to scream.

CHAPTER FOURTEEN

Gray Jenkins closed his eyes, as the scene unfolded before him. He did not want to relive the sights and sounds that he and his partner had witnessed at the river's edge. He began to tremble and look for ways to escape the debacle that was playing itself out in front of him. Etmus Sadiyo sat willing himself to move and take action. He was a police officer and thought himself trained for such moments. However, fear gripped him. He shook his head, trying to get the images out of his head. Flashes of light and empty shells of people raced through his mind.

He saw too much and knew too little. Etmus wanted answers but feared he was incapable of effectively dealing with the answers. Perhaps he needed to go back to church. His mother had taken him to church when he lived in Nevis, near the West Indies. She believed that God governed the world and that in Him there were answers to the deepest questions man can have. He had questions. He remembered his mother saying that the eyes were the windows to the soul. What happens when those windows appear as real glass, translucent and all revealing? Furthermore, what happens when someone looks into those windows and sees nothing but a dark abyss where life and living should be? Oh yes, he had questions.

Gray had some questions, as well. He wanted to know how he could get out of here without the guests realizing that he is a police officer and should be taking control of this situation. Many of the people had run out into the street, while others sat in stunned silence. Still, others were sobbing and whimpering like small children. It was a good thing that kids could not attend this function. He let out a silent prayer of thanks for that small consolation in this very big and ugly situation. He searched the mayhem looking for his girlfriend, Winter. His eyes scanned the hall and he realized the best man was consoling her. She had her head buried in his broad shoulders and he had his arms wrapped around her, protectively. He felt a twinge of jealousy at the way this man was holding his woman. She should have sought him for refuge, not Jarhys Houston.

He purposefully removed the thought from his head. He was not thinking clearly and besides what help could he have been to her when he could not get himself together. Jarhys was in closer proximity and there had been mild pandemonium when the lights came back on. There was no way she could have found her way to him in the midst of all of that. Still, to see the way Jarhys' hands moved up and down her back, and how comfortable she seemed ensconced in his arms, nagged at the back of his head.

"Someone should call 911," one of the guests whispered.

"There are firemen and police officers here already," someone else stated.

"Why the hell aren't they doing something?" A man questioned.

"A crime has been committed!" A woman screamed. "Do something!" She yelled to the unknown people who had sworn to uphold the law while protecting the community.

"What crime?"

"I don't know, but something isn't right. It's just not right!" The woman was getting hysterical.

"Everyone, try to calm down," Jackson Harris was speaking.

"Who are you?" A male voice asked.

"I am a Galena firefighter and rescue squad team member," he answered. "We need to assess the situation and find out what has happened."

"Is everyone accounted for?" Etmus found his voice.

The people in the hall began to look around to see who was missing.

"Some of the guests ran out of the hall when the lights came back on," someone said in the crowd.

"For those of you who came with someone who is not present inside the hall, please go outside and ask them to come back in. We need to get a head count."

Jackson walked over to Miles and put his hand on his shoulder. He could not imagine the pain his friend was experiencing right now. However, he needed Miles to focus and answer a few questions.

"How many people were invited who actually stated they would be in attendance?" Jackson inquired.

"About two hundred, Jacks," Miles answered. He was staring over in the direction of where Analise was last standing with her father.

"You should go to her, Miles."

"For what, Jacks?"

"She was about to become your wife, man."

"That woman over there is not the woman I was about to marry," Miles' voice grew louder. "That ...that ... that shell is ... that is not Analise."

A deep and grievous moan, rising from the pit of Evan Mitchell's being, erupted into the air in the hall. It filled the space and wrapped itself around everyone standing inside. They began to shake and cry, as his gut wrenching sobs reverberated off the rafters. He held himself, rocking back and forth and he cried. His tears spilled onto his face and down to the jacket of his tuxedo. They were big tears; tears filled with the pain from yesteryear. Tears he had not cried as he watched his daughter saturate her space with more and more in her attempt to fill her empty soul. He cried the tears of a father who could not give his daughter the substance she desperately needed, so he assuaged her requests for more, with more.

Katrice Mitchell, Analise's mother, sat in abject horror as she listened to the cries of her husband. She was unaccustomed to Evan not being in control of himself. Galia Fitzhugh rushed to her friend's side, as the Mayor of Galena took up the space next to the grieving father. He put his arm around his long-time friend and rocked with him. He did not want to know the pain this man was going through, but he wanted to support him in it. He would be there, in whatever capacity needed.

Ziva Montgomery was kneeling besides Analise praying. Her nursing skills were of no use at a time like this. She could only pray. She encouraged those around her who knew the power of prayer to begin to pray as well. Mitrice walked over to a corner, raised her arms and her eyes toward heaven and began to pray in the Spirit. Jackson walked along the outside aisle, praying as well. Galia and Phineas prayed as they manned the spot next to the parents of the bride. Adley Dane took his wife's hand and began to pray for the Mitchell family. Prayers swept throughout the hall, as people realized that was their only way to help. Pastor Montgomery stood at the podium and prayed into the microphone.

"Oh Lord, our God, we need You," he began.

Sirens blared over the prayers, as the paramedics and rescue squad made their way to Turner Hall in the center of Galena. Screeching tires and hurried voices mingled with the sound of prayer. Scurrying footsteps and the pushing of doors added accent to the petitions raised about the happenings of the day.

"There is no one that can make sense of this, without Your help," Pastor Montgomery continued.

The paramedics pushed past those who had rallied the courage to look at the body of Analise Mitchell, as she lay in front of her father.

"Father, please speak to us and give us direction. Come down and visit us during this grievous time. Grant peace to those who have been deeply wounded by what has taken place within these walls."

The gurney rested on the floor and the rescue squad members looked at each other, as they contemplated their next move. Ordinarily, it would have been a simple task to place the body on the gurney and rush it out into the waiting truck.

"Oh God, touch the hearts and minds of the family members, the wedding party and most urgently the groom. He needs You more than ever, dear Lord."

Ghrelin scanned the room to see if he could catch sight of Mavet. He had some questions, himself, and he was going to demand some answers. However, he was nowhere in sight. The prayers of the people were grating on his ears. They were too loud and it was giving him a headache. Why did no one come to his side? Analise was his friend, too. He was as confused and hurt as the next person was. Why were the church people not looking to console him? Just then, Axel Fitzhugh was at his side.

"Dude, this is too much to deal with," Axel said to Ghrelin.

Ghrelin turned and looked into Axel's face. He felt a sense of relief to have someone he was familiar with to be here with him in this moment.

"I had no idea you knew the bride and groom," Axel looked around nervously.

How could he be unaffected by the chaos in the room? Ghrelin scanned the hall looking for Mavet. He was visibly nowhere.

"And the parents of this young lady, God…draw them closer to You and show them what the other needs during this time. Do not allow them to withdraw from one another or from You. They need one another more than ever and You are the bond that will keep them while they search for answers."

Ghrelin put his hands to his ears. He could not understand why this pastor was praying so loudly into the microphone. He could not hear himself think. His head was pounding and he was feeling weak. Even Axel seemed affected by the clamor; he was rubbing his hands together and swaying from side to side. Ghrelin needed Axel to calm down and maybe he could get himself together, too. He began to talk to him about what his plans were; wanted to see if he still needed more free time to get his head together after school.

Axel was grateful for the distraction Ghrelin provided him. He concentrated on his voice and was able to fight off the urge to do something. Besides, what could he do in the midst of this madness? He did not want to get in the way. The paramedics were on the scene, there were law enforcement officers and a firefighter here; and there was no reason for him to get involved. But, as Pastor Zeke was praying, he felt like he should come to the aid of someone. There were so many people dazed and confused who sat alone. As Ghrelin spoke, the pressure was easing up. Axel needed some assistance, and no one was coming to help him out. It was just Ghrelin. Therefore, he turned his full attention to his friend and gave up the notion that he had something to offer.

"Thank You, Father, for giving people the heart to help those in need. So many, in this room, are hurting and confused; they are in need of direction."

"Then why isn't he helping them?" Axel asked Ghrelin. "Why is he just standing up there praying and not offering his assistance to those around him?"

Ghrelin agreed. He did not understand why the pastor was expecting others to do something he was unwilling to do himself. What did he think his praying was doing? It was incessant chatter, as far as he was concerned. The pastor stands at the microphone spouting out words and commands to others to help. He could see that Axel was struggling with the whole thing. All this kid wanted was to be left alone to do what kids do. He did not want the responsibility of having to come to the rescue of grown people.

Ghrelin moved closer to Axel and put his arm around him. *The poor boy*, he thought.

Galia looked across the aisle, at her son. "Axel, are you alright?"

"What do you want me to do, Mom?"

"Axel, are you alright?" Galia asked, again.

"I'm not prepared to do anything – what do I know?"

Galia could not leave her friend, now, but she knew her son was in trouble. She looked around, frantically, trying to see whom she could ask to assist her child. Phineas was still holding Evan, Pastor Zeke was praying and almost everyone else was assisting others.

"Axel…"

"Mom, stop asking me to do something. I cannot do anything for these people. I am fine, right where I am," Axel's voice cracked.

Ghrelin knew what Axel needed; someone to tell him it was okay to be still. He did not need his mother asking him questions. He did not need the pressure of feeling obligated to go to someone's aid. He needed to just sit in his chair and do nothing. Couldn't his mother see what her son was going through? Something tragic has just happened and it is a lot to process for a young man. Besides, Axel was helping him.

Ziva could feel another force, at work, in the room. As she prayed, the Holy Spirit was speaking to her heart. He confirmed what she has suspected since the day she went back to work; a spiritual force had taken up residence in Galena. She kept hearing the Spirit say the word 'BEHOLDEN'. A spirit of antichrist had come to collect an owed debt. She was not clear as to what that meant, but now she knew where to focus her consecration and fast. There was a sense of urgency, in the spirit realm, and she understood there was no time to waste. She would have to talk to Zeke about this. The intercessors needed to be put on alert, high alert. They needed to establish a prayer line so that someone was praying around the clock.

The paramedics put Analise Mitchell's body on the gurney and advised her father that they would be taking her to the heliport to transfer her to Mercy Medical Center in Dubuque. They had room for one person to accompany her, in the ambulance and helicopter, but no more. Evan could not leave his wife, nor could he have her traveling alone with their daughter. Ziva volunteered to accompany Analise during the transport, while Phineas and Galia would drive the two of them to the hospital.

As the rescue team made their way out of Turner Hall and into the awaiting ambulance, someone escorted Evan and Katrice Mitchell to the Fitzhugh's car. Etmus Sadiyo was making his way around the room to speak with those who were capable. Gray Jenkins walked over to retrieve his woman from the arms of Jarhys

Houston. Maren Dane slipped her hand out of her husband's when she thought she saw him watching First Lady Ziva walk out of the door. Miles Kirkpatrick sat down in the chair next to a dazed and tearful Alaina Toussaint. Jackson Harris made his way to the corner where Mitrice Reynolds knelt in prayer. Axel Fitzhugh remained in his seat next to a preoccupied Ghrelin. Pastor Zeke Montgomery continued to pray.

Mavet stood in the doorway of the hall watching the people. He knew some of his friends could really use his assistance, at this moment. He looked over at Maren Dane. She was shrinking into herself, as she believed her husband was lusting after the pastor's wife. She sought his solace with answers that only he could give her. She was desperate to have what Ziva Montgomery had - beauty, confidence, a loving husband and family. *If only …*

CHAPTER FIFTEEN

Katriel did not know what was going on in her world. Everything seemed to up in the air. Her father had done one of his disappearing acts and her mother was beginning to worry. She had no idea why her mom would be so concerned about a man who does not love her, but she has been staying up nights praying for him. She had to admit that the atmosphere in the house has been calmer since her dad left. She hoped he was gone for good. She was certain they would be better off, if he did not step foot back into the house. However, she was not so sure that her mother would survive the abandonment. As terrible as her father was, her mother still wanted her marriage; still believed that things would turn around. She hated to say it, yet she was beginning to feel like her mother was not as strong as she first hoped. What self-respecting woman would pine over someone who treated her the way her mom was treated? *"God, please do not let me make the same mistakes,"* she silently prayed.

Her cell phone was vibrating, on her nightstand. She looked at the clock and wondered who would be calling her this close to midnight. She reached for it and pushed 'talk' on the screen.

"Hello," Katriel answered.

"Katriel, has your father come home?" It was Marissa Montgomery.

"No. Why?"

Marissa sighed, on the other end of the phone. She did not know how to explain to her friend the weird feeling she was getting about her father not coming home. She knew he was prone to moments of absence, but she was sensing something, else. She had been praying about her friend and her family. It hurt her to see that Katriel was so unhappy, when she was at home. She knew her father was abusive and that he had issues with anger. She had asked God if He would see fit for Mr. Palmer to seek counseling for his issue, but that never happened. Marissa imagined that there was another plan because she could not perceive that God would have Mrs. Palmer and Katriel suffer at the hands of an angry man.

"I am beginning to think that something is not kosher about your dad's absence."

"What do you mean?"

"Well, I was praying and I got a feeling that there was more to him not being home than him just walking away, as he had done in the past."

"Marissa, what are you talking about?"

"You know that I have been praying for you and your family; especially since we talked that day in the library."

"Yes, and I appreciate that."

"Yeah, well, I got a sense that your father's disappearance was not voluntary."

"You think something actually happened to my dad? What makes you think that, Marissa?"

"I don't know how to explain it. I just think that something is going on, in this town, and your father may have gotten in the middle of it, somehow."

"Marissa, of course if something is going on in this town, my father is in the middle of it; he is the chief of police."

"I am not talking about physical criminal activity. I am referring to something less apparent. I just do not have a good feeling about it, Katriel."

The more she talked the less she was making sense to herself. How was she going to get her friend to understand that there really may be some demonic activity going on, right here in their town? She began to feel it necessary to take her relationship, with God, more seriously. When she prayed more and read her bible more, she started getting the notion that another spirit was at work in the lives of people. Things were looking a bit black and white when it came to the things of God. Either you chose God and His way of doing things or you chose your own way of doing things. She watched a lot of the adults in the church confess that they were Christians; which means to be Christ-like. However, many of them went about their lives as they deemed fit. It was as if they enjoyed the look of being churchgoers than the actual commitment to being true believers. She didn't want to be that way.

Marissa continued, "Do you remember hearing, on the news, about a man who simply vanished off the Galena River Trail?"

"Yes, my father was investigating that disappearance."

"Well, I read in the paper that there is speculation that this isn't a simple disappearance; people are thinking the man is dead."

"What are you trying to say, Marissa? You think my father is dead?" Katriel began to get a sick feeling in the pit of her stomach.

Marissa did not answer the question.

"I, also, heard that the day your father did not come home that there was some kind of situation that happened down by the river's edge."

"And…"

"The river's edge is at the end of the Galena Trail, Katriel."

"Wait a minute. How did you hear about that?"

"You know Patterson, from school?"

"Yeah."

"Well, he interns down at the Gazette and one of the journalists has been camped out at the station trying to get news about the disappearance of that guy."

"And…"

"And, she was in the station when your father stormed out after the police officers that he put in charge of the case. He was spouting off saying something about having to take care of things himself."

Katriel thought it was just like her father to go off half-cocked in a rage, thinking he was the only one who could handle things. She could see him, now, in his officer garb racing down his own men to do their job. She shook her head. To think, he was saying how glad he was not to be on the street chasing down criminals.

"Why are you just now saying something to me, Marissa?" Katriel asked.

"Well, you insisted that your father's absence was just another one of his trips and that he would be home within the week."

"Oh my God, I had not even thought about the fact that he has been gone for so long!"

"Katriel, we need to pray for your father."

"What if it is too late? What if God answered my prayers and my father is dead? What if this is my fault?" Katriel felt herself begin to hyperventilate.

"Calm down, Katriel. This is bigger than your moment of anger against your dad; sure that needs to be addressed, but this is more."

"My mother will never forgive me."

"Stop thinking about yourself and focus, Katriel; this is bigger than you. I heard my mother praying, one day, I can't remember when exactly. But, she was asking God to show her what was going on in the area. Then I realized that what I had been sensing was on point."

"Marissa, what am I going to do? What are we going to do if something has happened to my father?" Katriel could not believe what she was saying. Wasn't she just saying how they would be better off without him? Obviously, she did not believe it. She realized that she was not being the best Christian she can be, while judging her father. She should have been praying for him, not wishing he were dead.

"Katriel, we need to get a group of teenagers who are serious about God and pray for our families and this town. Ever since we talked at the library, I have been asking God to show me what is at the heart of things. First, I had to deal with me. I didn't want to be pointing the finger at others and all the while things were off in my own life."

"You sound like one of the old church mothers," Katriel let out a weak laugh.

"I know, but I respect my mother and her relationship with God. She never allows a day to pass without taking the time to check in – to ask that He direct her day, and not just direct it by the plans she has made. It sounds weird, but I think I understand it, now."

"Well, explain it to me."

"I am not talking about not setting goals for yourself or having a vision for where you would like your life to go. I hope to graduate, next year, and continue on to Michigan University to study law. I have plans. But, like my mother says, will you leave a task undone that isn't on *your* agenda to continue on the path set by yourself?"

"Something like when that guy in the bible was heading on a journey and someone came to him for help; he set his plan aside to help this man, and then continued on to his destination."

"Yes! Nothing that we plan should supersede a God moment; a time when we can show someone God by doing what He did; give up a part of ourselves for the sake of the greater good. If someone knew we were headed in the opposite direction and we chose to walk with them instead, so they would not be alone."

"That makes sense."

"It does! But, in order for us to be sensitive enough to know when a God moment has presented itself, we need to be serious about God."

"True."

"So, with all of this activity going on around us, we need to pray."

"Okay. Okay. I understand."

"Good. So, tomorrow after church, let's get with the teenagers that seem serious and start a prayer and bible study group."

"Who's going to be the leader?"

"We can decide if we need one when we talk with the others."

"Makes sense."

"In the meantime, we need to pray for your dad."

"And my mom, too."

Nora lay in her bed, staring up at the ceiling. She reached her arm out to the side of the bed normally occupied by Gavin. She missed his presence in their bed. She missed the warmth of his body as she nuzzled close to him, after he had fallen asleep. She did not have any grand notions about her marriage being picture perfect, but it was her marriage. Gavin was her choice and she was determined to live without regrets. She was a grown woman who had lost the gift of childlike faith in humankind. How ironic it seemed, in this moment, to be a pediatric cardiologist and not have the heart of a child to believe that the best will prevail?

She sighed. Sleep was going to evade her, as it has over the past several days. The emptiness of her bed was more than she wanted to deal with, at this time. She swung her legs to the floor and slid her slippers on her feet. She walked over to the small sofa by the balcony window and sat down. Nora sighed, again. She wanted to be present for Katriel, but it was apparent that her daughter had lost respect for her. She was a poor example of what it meant to be a strong African American woman. She remained in a loveless marriage that has turned bitter and abusive.

No matter the condition of their marriage, there remained a glimmer of hope. She could not find the source of the tiny flickering flame, but she sensed its presence. She did not believe that Gavin loved her, but somehow her love for him remained. Throughout the years, she knew that he felt a forced imprisonment, married to her. He was not ready to settle down when she got pregnant, but he did it to quell her fears. She did not want to face a world that would judge her because she fell in love and got herself knocked up. Therefore, Gavin chose her over himself and did the right thing; or at least what she thought was the right thing. If she had known then, what she knows now … She let the thought fall to the ground. Going back over it now was not going to change reality. She opened her legs to a man that did not love her and she was living with the result of her foolishness.

However, she had to be honest and say that it was not all bad. Nothing is *all* of anything; that was something that her grandmother repeated to her, often. There is only one constant in the universe and that is God. He is the only *all, ever* and *never*; humanity falls in the middle. She would say that we are very *gray area* creatures. The one thing that we could count on human nature being is mutable. We are the variable and God is the constant. She would insist that Nora make a conscious effort to remember that. This is what kept ringing in her mind when Gavin would have his mood swings. She was to try to remember that when she could not depend on her husband to be concerned about her well-being that God was always concerned. In addition, when the times arose that she began to doubt that truth, she would get a gentle reminder, most of the time, in the form of her beautiful daughter.

Katriel is her precious gift from God, an angel whom God entrusted to her. Moreover, even when Gavin could not stand the sight of her, in the early days, she would see his face light up when he would look at their daughter. It was in those moments that she would remember why she fell in love with him. His eyes would soften, as well as the lines in his face. She spent many days standing in the doorway, out of view, and watch the two of them. She would long for *that* Gavin to be present when they were alone. It was *that* Gavin whom she wanted to return home.

She could hear Katriel talking on the phone. She glanced over at the clock on the bedside table. Her brow furrowed wondering whom her daughter could be talking to at this time of night. She walked toward the door, intending on going into her bedroom. She stopped in her tracks. It sounded like her daughter was praying. Tears welled up in Nora's eyes. She stood in her doorway listening to her baby praying for her father, their family and the people of Galena. She felt a prick in her heart. She should have been praying instead of sitting around moping and feeling sorry for herself. God had given her peace when there was none found all around her. The thought of His pervasive love is what kept her putting one foot in front of the other when the weight of her life pressed her down.

She closed her door and fell to her knees. She needed God's consistency, in this moment when it felt like her footing was on shifting sand.

"God, I am sorry," Nora began as the tears flowed freely down her face.

———————————————

John Doe number two began to stir. Mavet's head popped up and he rose from the chair. He walked over to the bed and touched his hand. He had not moved since the day they brought him to the hospital. His eyes flickered, as if they might have opened. He became restless and agitated. The machines began to go haywire and the intensive care nurse rushed into the room. She brushed past Mavet in order to check his vitals and reset the machine. Mavet wondered what was going on. Was John Doe number two fighting to recover?

Mavet felt the atmosphere change in the room. It was charged and electrified. He felt his composure fading because he did not know what was going on, and he had no control over it. He moved his eyes from the bed to the door. What was this force and where was it coming from? It had not been in this room before. He looked up as he heard commotion in the hall...it was Ziva Montgomery and she escorted Analise Mitchell onto the intensive care floor. Mavet left the room.

CHAPTER SIXTEEN

People were standing outside of the Wisdom Outreach Center before the doors opened. There were hushed conversations taking place while parishioners and visitors, alike, patiently waited to enter into the sanctuary. When Pastor Zeke and First Lady Ziva drove up, they were surprised to see so many already there. They looked at each other, while Marissa looked out of the window.

"Whoa!" Marissa exclaimed.

"I'll say," First Lady Ziva added.

"God is good," Pastor Zeke stated, in a relieved tone.

"I am sure this has to do with the scare at the wedding," Ziva said.

"And the fact that so many people have come up missing," Marissa offered.

"No matter the cause, thank God for the people."

Pastor Zeke Montgomery had been waiting for this moment since he began in ministry. He wanted to see people lining up to come into his services; ready to hear what God wanted to say to His people. He hoped he had the answers to the many questions that had to be swirling around in the minds of those at the wedding and other townspeople. He had gotten word from one of the deacons that Sofia Koen, Levi's wife, had gone missing. He came home from work to find the kids indoors and the patio door wide open. Tragic.

As he parked the car, his armor bearer came up to it to open the door for the first family of the Wisdom Outreach Center. A somber look blanketed his face. He whispered into Zeke's ear, as Ziva and Marissa walked into the church. The pastor was troubled. Something had begun to gnaw at the back of his head. Yet, he shook it off; he did not want to become distracted and be ineffective during the sermon, this morning.

Amongst those waiting to go into the church, was Mavet. He stood alone, this morning. His usual companions were not in the crowd. He did notice Ghrelin and Axel talking to one another, near the middle of the throng of people. He turned to look at those who turned out because trouble was brewing in the town. He chuckled, to himself. Humankind was a funny lot. When things are good, they tend to throw off the notion of God and His providence. They live their lives in the fear and admonition of society and mass media, until the unexplainable happens. Then, they turn to the man of the cloth, or woman, to dish them out beautiful plates of explanations that will alleviate their acute stress. Once done, they will go back to life as usual; self-directed and desire motivated. Mavet heard Pastor Zeke call that kind of person carnal minded, only seeking that which gratifies their souls and not their spirits.

Babette and Cale Richmond were at the end of the line because they were just returning to town from their trip to the Palace Campgrounds. They were puzzled that they would have to stand in line before entering the building. They looked around to see if there was a familiar face, in the crowd, but could not find one. Cale stepped out into the street to get a better view and he noticed Mavet scanning the crowd, as well. He waved for him to come up to where he stood in the line. He motioned for his wife and kids to follow him to where Mavet was standing.

Mavet tried to get Cale up to speed on the happenings in the town since he left on his mini-vacation with the family. He told him about Sofia Koen and her disappearance. Cale advised that he knew something was going on when his wife came home, stating that Ms. Koen did not meet her when she went to pick up the kids. A teenager from the neighborhood was at the house, and told her that the Koens were unavailable and had hired her to sit with the kids until she came. Mavet told him about yesterday's wedding, and how paramedics rushed Analise Mitchell to Mercy Medical Center after collapsing at the altar. There was also word that Adley Dane reported his wife missing after the fiasco at Turner Hall.

Cale could not believe that so much had taken place in such a short amount of time. He began to worry about his family and their safety. What if there was some maniac on the loose, kidnapping people, or worse. Hadn't the chief of police gone missing or was presumed missing? He thought he overheard some of the officers talking about it in the halls of the circuit court. What must his poor wife and daughter be dealing with, at this moment? There was also the original missing person's case, earlier this month.

The crowd was beginning to move and file into the church. The ushers and deacons greeted each person with a warm smile and handshake, before directing them to their seats. They had to open the balcony and the overflow room in order to accommodate all the people. It seemed as if the whole town decided to come to the Wisdom Outreach Center, this morning. They could not imagine what the other churches were doing and if they had to handle such a large crowd.

The worship and praise team were in rare form as they realized they had a bigger audience. People clapped their hands and sang along while the soloist and choir members bellowed out popular hymns. Mavet noticed there were quite a few of the members who had put down their Blackberry's and iPhones, this Sunday. They were not so concerned about social media and business emails, today. He shook his head. He wondered what they hoped to glean from the service this morning that Zeke had not been spouting over the years. Many of them entertained fear and anxiety. These were the existentialists, people looking for explanations and guidance from someone they thought to be an authority figure for the pressure they were experiencing due to the upheaval in their lives.

Mavet chose to sit with Cale and his family, today. They had some catching up to do because he had been busy, and the judge was away getting some quality family time. During the singing portion of the service, the two of them chatted about his caseload at the circuit court, as well as how he could hear more cases to gain notice from other districts. They talked about a seat becoming available in Iowa and one in Wisconsin along with whether it would be a good move for him to put his bid in. Cale was apprehensive about uprooting his young family and taking his wife away from the big project she had been working on. Mavet advised that both municipalities were not too far away from Galena; and if he had to go while his family stayed, he could always return on the weekends.

Cale began to contemplate the idea, seriously. He also thought of the new faces, and paralegals, he would see. He conjured up images of the delicacies he could sample being away from his wife and home. He reached behind his wife to caress her bottom, gently. She giggled, swiped his hand away and gave him a look that told him they would have time for this later. He put his hand around her waist and smiled. He loved his wife.

"Good morning, everyone," Ziva Montgomery was on the podium.

Mavet wanted to suck his teeth and roll his eyes. He knew he was being childish, but he could not help it. Ziva really got under his skin. Moreover, this morning, he could not get anyone to aid in his attempt to zone her out because all eyes were up front. He sat down as everyone else stood in respect to the First Lady. He wanted her out of his hair. He remained annoyed by her commanding presence last night at the hospital. He had never felt the need to leave his friend, even when she had been in the area. He knew she had been on a consecration and that always added power to her.

"It is good to see so many faces in the congregation, today," she began.

"It is with a heavy heart and spirit that I stand before you, this morning. Galena is in crisis, church."

Many of the crowd yelled out "amen" while others used another form of agreement. They felt a sense of camaraderie amongst themselves, as they gave verbal assent to what was being said. The people did not want to feel alone in their fear and it gave them a form of comfort to know that someone in authority could give voice to their feelings.

"We need to rally together and pray. The demonic oppression that has shrouded our community is striking too close for comfort. This spiritual assault has targeted many members of the Wisdom Outreach Center. We need the intercessors, the wailing women and mighty men of valor to take up the assignment and get on the wall."

A thunderous applause met her impassioned call to arms. Marissa nudged Katriel and they nodded their heads. It caused them to smile knowing that they had not been off course when they were speaking, last night. They looked down the row to see if the other teenagers had been listening. All eyes were on the podium.

Jarhys Houston felt his cell phone vibrating in is pants pocket, but refused to answer it. He was still shook by the turn of events at his best friend's wedding. He noticed that quite a few people from the wedding were in attendance, this morning; including Winter Pharron and her beau Gray Jenkins. Etmus Sadiyo, the officer gathering information was there with his brother Jackson Harris. The wedding planner, Mitrice Reynolds was sitting with the brothers.

Adley Dane sat in the congregation with a heavy heart. The oppression had crept into his home; his darling wife, Maren, had gone missing after the paramedics left with Analise. He had been feeling like she was unhappy in the marriage for quite some time, but did not think that she wanted to leave. Usually weddings gave couples the opportunity to think back on their special day, but Maren seemed distant. He had been praying, as instructed, and wanted his wife to be in agreement with the prayer. Her hand lay limp in his while he prayed, until she finally slipped it out. He loved his wife and hoped she would return to him. He kept pushing away the nagging feeling that something else happened to his beloved. Her purse remained in the seat next to him, as was her cell phone and hat. So much was going on, yesterday, that he had not noticed her leave.

Zeke Montgomery stepped out onto the podium to join his wife. He took her hand in his as he took his place next to her on the rostrum. They were a powerhouse, together; a formidable spiritual force as they stood in agreement. She smiled, as he leaned in to kiss her on the forehead.

"Isn't she beautiful folks?" He asked.

The congregations clapped and cheered.

"What a blessing to have her stand with me, in the ministry. She loves the Lord and she loves His people. WOC is lucky to have her and so am I."

"You better say it, Pastor!" someone yelled from the audience.

"I will never stop saying it. She has been in prayer for each, and every one, of you, even those of you who are visiting. Galena and the outlying counties have been heavy on her heart and she has turned her plate down to seek the Lord on behalf of you all. In fact, we both have," Pastor Zeke went on.

He felt Ziva stiffen beside him, but she did not move or allow the expression on her face to change. Mavet perked up. He moved to the front of the church to be closer to the pastor. He knew he needed him, in this moment. He was not going to get the support he, so desperately, needed from Ziva right about now. He stood where the leader of the church could see him. He gave him a nod to let him know that he had his support. He gave him the thumbs-up sign to encourage him to continue speaking to the people.

Pastor Zeke felt a twinge of pain in his sternum, but he would not allow minor discomfort to ruin this moment. His church was filled to capacity. He knew there were members of the congregation that have been going through some difficult times. Maddock Hamilton, Gavin Palmer, Sofia Koen, Analise Mitchell and Maren Dane were all members of the Wisdom Outreach Center, and they are affected by whatever is going on. The pain was growing more intense as he began to realize that everyone touched by the demonic activity were his parishioners. He could not catch his breath for a moment, but he rallied through his statement to the church.

Her husband's lie puzzled Ziva, but she was even more concerned about his apparent discomfort. The more he talked the more labored his breathing sounded to her. It was obvious that it was not evident to those in the audience, but she felt him tense up. She wanted to get him seated and question him about what was going on with him.

"It is offering time in the sanctuary," Zeke finally spoke.

The deacons followed their cue, as usual, and began to hand out envelopes for those who were willing to give in the morning offering. While that was taking place, Zeke and Ziva walked over to their seats. He rubbed his chest and grimaced, as the pain increased in intensity.

"What is going on, Zeke," Ziva whispered.

"I don't know. I have this crushing pain in my sternum that worsens when I attempt to take a deep breath," Zeke described.

"Do you need to go to the hospital?"

"I will be fine, baby girl. The show must go on."

"Zeke, do you hear yourself?"

"Ziva, I have wanted nothing more for this ministry than to have more people."

"I know, Zeke, but at what cost?" she questioned.

"At all cost," he looked incredulous. How could she not know his ambitions?

"Zeke, you are sounding greedy; greedy for God's people."

"Ziva, it is a sign of an effective ministry when a pastor can amass great numbers."

"I showed you all these things, that working in this way we ought to help those being weak, and remember the words of the Lord Jesus, that He said, 'It is more blessed to give than to receive.'"

"What…"

"Acts chapter twenty verse thirty-five; where that word, *lambano,* can mean to receive. But, Zeke, it can also mean to take hold of or seize. It is a greedy spirit that is more apt to seize than to give. You are looking to take hold of God's people more than you are willing to give to them."

"Ziva, that is preposterous!" Zeke whispered roughly. "I have done nothing but give the people what God has given me. I am endeavoring to give more for more of God's people." He rubbed his chest.

"It started out that way, Zeke Montgomery, but now you have made more people an idol to look up to and to sacrifice for and that is not what this ministry was founded on."

Mavet had come to stand next to Pastor Zeke. He leaned in and whispered into his ear. He knew he needed someone who was on his side, someone who knew what he was trying to do with the Wisdom Outreach Center. He knew that if he had a greater turnout of congregants that he would be able to do more work and he would get the nod from other mega churches. He put his hand on his shoulder and the pain in Zeke's chest compounded. He leaned back in his chair and closed his eyes.

Ziva could feel the foul stench of antichrist near her husband. She knew what she needed to do. She heard God saying, "*Woe, woe, the great city, she who was clothed in fine linen and purple and scarlet, and adorned with gold and precious stones and pearls;"*

"Zeke, honey, God is warning that this has turned into something other than worship. It looks good and sounds good, but it is like the city of Babylon, a form of godliness. Do not allow your greed for people to overshadow God's glory."

Zeke patted her hand and smiled at his wife.

"I got this."

Zeke stood up to pray for the offering, as was his custom. He reached out for Ziva's hand and helped her to her feet. They walked to the podium and just before he spoke, he clutched his chest. He stumbled and Ziva put her arm around him to keep him from falling to the ground. His armor bearer ran over to assist the First Lady as she tried to get him back to the seat. The congregation began speak in hushed tones, as they watched the scene play out in front of them. Mavet was at Zeke's side, as well. He was intent on remaining by his side, through this ordeal.

"Ahhhhh!" Zeke yelled, as the searing pain ripped through his sternum and into his back.

Marissa ran up on the podium to see what was going on with her father. She knelt in front of him and her mother rubbed her hair. Ziva was worried about her husband, but she was more in tune with the Spirit of God, in this moment. Darkness had invaded the hallowed halls of the Wisdom Outreach Center. She heard God say that people were giving place to their vices and He needed true worship and heartfelt prayer so the ministering flames of fire could come and do the bidding of His people.

Zeke felt himself losing consciousness because his breaths were becoming too difficult to take because of the crushing pain. He gasped and grabbed his chest. Fear crept into his heart, as he thought about his mortality.

In the same instant, both Ziva and Marissa Montgomery yelled out, "Pray church!"

CHAPTER SEVENTEEN

The line seemed to go on endlessly. No one was talking, as everyone walked sullenly along the sidewalk. A lone ashen concrete block building was the only structure in the near vicinity. There were no cars, trucks or buses traversing the street, yet there was a traffic light swinging overhead. The sky was gray, like a fresh rain had recently fallen, but the ground was dry. The cracks in the cement showed the only signs of color with sprigs of dying grass pushing up through them. Every person in the line hung their heads, as if shame was weighing them down. As the people moved along, there was the sound of clinking chains and dragging cinderblocks. It was in that moment, that the man realized that his hands were chained and the chains were attached to large blocks of stone.

He attempted to speak to the person in front of him; however, no words sounded. He began to panic and fight against the chains and the involuntary muteness. It was all to no avail. Trapped, he could not call for help. His eyes darted around, looking for some sign or clue as to where he was and how he could break free. *"No need to try, it's useless."* The forlorn voice was in his head. He wanted to know what was going on and how he became chained to this line, in the first place. He had no idea how long he had been there – it seemed as if he just woke up, in this line.

Maybe this is all a dream. A sick and demented dream and he was going to wake up any minute. *"It's no use. This is not a dream."* There was that voice, again, feeding him the same melancholy answers. *"I have fought against the chains until my wrists became raw; or at least they feel that way."* The man in front of him looked down at his wrists. How could this be? It seemed to him like the man in front of him was communicating by way of some sort of telepathy. He wondered if he could do it and get some answers; answers that he wanted and not this doom and gloom bull zapped into his brain. In addition, he wanted to know where this line headed.

"From what I can tell, it just leads beyond that door. It is too dark past the threshold to see anything else."

"How long have you been here? How long have I been here?" There, he did it! So he thought, but he did not get any message that answered his direct questions. Perhaps this only worked when he was thinking to himself. It could be that this weirdo was some mind reading hustler.

"*I wasn't always a weirdo,*" he began. "*I was successful, had a beautiful girlfriend and was training for one of the biggest races of my career.*"

The line moved, the chains clank and the stone weights dragged. He realized that he was not moving of his volition. There was a force pulling them along, like the moving passageways at the airports. He wondered how he could hear the boulders moving and the chains clinking, if they were not actually moving their arms and legs.

"*If you look down you will realize that the stones which the chains are attached to sit just outside of where your legs are; so when you are moved they drag.*"

He looked down and verified that the communication was the truth. He also noticed that there was some sort of lettering on his stones. He looked toward the man's stones and saw he had some, as well. They did not look like the same letters carved into his blocks. He tried to bend down to see what it was; however, he could not.

"No need to keep trying that. You will only be able to move head and upper body. You are no longer in control of your own body."

It seemed like he was in control of nothing. He had no voluntary movements. He was being propelled along, against his will, through a door that led to God knows where. God … he remembered hearing about God; he even went to church. It made him angry to think that God would allow this sort of thing to go on under His heaven.

"God has nothing to do with this place, it seems. In my mind, I perceive this place as a self-induced hell. Have you realized that your most ardent emotions keep replaying in your mind?"

Funny that he would say that. The only reel that kept replaying in his mind was being angry. There was nothing else. He was angry about everything. He was angry that he was in this soup line with this Houdini of the mind. He was angry that he had bound hands and that he no longer had a voice.

"*It seems that your emotion of choice was anger, then*," the voice stated matter-of-factly.

In that moment, the man in front of him was whisked through the door. What did he mean emotion of choice? No one chooses their emotions; the people around them thrust them upon them. Why would he choose to be enraged at the slightest things? What did he have to gain from the fury that welled up on the inside of him every time he encountered the ineptness of those around him? He was forced to be angry.

"*You enjoyed being angry*," this time it was a female voice in his head. "*Your anger helped you get your way. It was used as a manipulative tool. You were an intimidator; a low-life bully.*"

Whom was this woman speaking down to him? Last, he saw, she was in the same line with the rest of them. She had no right to demean him or attempt to belittle him. His community, his home and in his church respected him. In addition, when he got beyond this mysterious doorway, he was going to get the answers he sought. He would demand it!

"We'll see about that. It doesn't seem like you will have much say in this place. Look, they have you chained like a dog and they have stolen your voice. Just think about that."

The pulley began to move, his chains rattle and the accompanying boulder dragged as something propelled him beyond the door and into a room. The air was stagnate and stale in the small space. A dim light seemed to be coming from a lone candle in the corner. He squinted and thought he could make out a small makeshift pallet on the floor, across from where he landed. There was no other piece of furniture. He was not sure he would be able to make his way to the cushions, but he tried anyway. To his surprise, he had free range of motion, as long as he could drag the boulder around. He did not think this would be a problem, in this confined area. He walked over and sat down. He leaned his head against the cement wall and closed his eyes.

"You are all around me. You are behind me and in front of me. You hold me in your power.

I'm amazed at how well you know me. It's more than I can understand. How can I get away from Your Spirit? Where can I go to escape from you? If I go up to the heavens, you are there. If I lie down in the deepest parts of the earth, you are also there. Suppose I were to rise with the sun in the east and then cross over to the west where it sinks into the ocean. Your hand would always be there to guide me. Your right hand would still be holding me close. Suppose I were to say, I'm sure the darkness will hide me. The light around me will become as dark as night. Even that darkness would not be dark to you. The night would shine like the day, because darkness is like light to you."

Ziva Montgomery refused to allow this attack to distract her from her assignment. With Zeke in the intensive care unit at Mercy Medical Center, it added fodder to the flame of intercession. She walked into each room and repeated the hundred and thirty-ninth psalm. She was going to speak life to every John and Jane Doe that had come through these doors. She was speaking life to her husband. He seemed to have lost his way, for a moment. She was not going to let it end this way. She was prepared to do battle, on any field necessary to get her man and his spirit back. And, why not bring everyone else with him?

She surrounded this floor with prayer and the Word of God. Analise Mitchell was still in her coma after her intestines ruptured the day of her wedding. There were two other women, Jane Does brought in, around the same time. One had a life threatening heart infection and the other had bone cancer that was causing her bones to rot, from the inside out. The two John Does were still there, as well. John Doe number two, with the necrotizing liver condition seemed to improve a little, but his face was still distorted and unrecognizable. Then there was her love, lying sedated in that room with what the doctors called Tietze's syndrome; she was more familiar with the term costochondritis. There was inflammation of the juncture of cartilage that joined the breastbone to the rib bone, his sternum. The doctor said that those likely to reproduce repetitive micro-movements or the actions performed by professional rowers were the main cause of the situation.

Zeke had an aggressive form of the condition and doctors asked Ziva if her husband had been pulling heavy objects toward his sternum, regularly. She asked if it could have been from working out on weighted gym equipment. The doctor stated he would have had to been doing extensive training in order for this much swelling to be present. They sedated him to keep him out of pain and required he be in intensive care in case the swelling caused pressure on his vital organs - mainly the heart and lungs.

Marissa had been staying with Nora Palmer and her daughter Katriel while she stayed at the hospital with Zeke. She wanted to be here when he was able to come off the medication and talk to her. In the meantime, she fasted and prayed for everyone on the floor. She prayed for the congregation. She prayed for their community. Nevertheless, more than anything, she prayed for her husband. She had been terrified that Sunday when he collapsed. She thought he was having a heart attack. She could not envision herself without this man. She told God, as much. Jaden and Marissa needed their father and she needed her husband. He was the love of her life and she wanted to spend the rest of her life loving him, in the land of the living.

She walked back into his room and sat in the chair next to his bed. She took his hand and kissed it. Tears fell down her face as she looked at her man. She adored his deep brown skin, especially when it contrasted against her milky complexion. She often told him that Marissa was a perfect blend of the two of them, a strong coffee with just the right amount of cream. They made beautiful children together. She could have had seven more, if it was God's will. She loved being the incubator for his seed. With each passing day of her pregnancy, she grew more in love with him. She could not get enough of him and he knew how to take care of her.

"I need you, Zeke Montgomery. I need you like I need the blood coursing through my veins."

Ziva put her forehead on her husband's arm. The touch of his skin always made her feel better. Her hair fell against him and he stirred. She looked up to see if he was trying to open his eyes. But, he wasn't. She did what she knew to do; she prayed.

"Most Gracious God, my Father - I come to you, today, giving you all the honor and glory due your name. You are Master of the universe - Sovereign ruler of all of the heavens and earth. You sit high and You look low, forever concerning yourself with Your creation. I make Your name great, in the earth. I will always declare Your awesome wonders to all who will listen. You intend to manifest Your blessings and favor upon Your people, Your chosen ones - the apple of Your eye - You have us engraved on the palms of both Your hands, never to leave or forsake us. Your mercy is from everlasting to everlasting - and Your grace encompasses us, like a robe - You have crowned us with Your loving kindness, and encamped us roundabout with ministering angels, like flames of fire. It is by Your command that the sun rises and sets - You declare when the tide rolls in and goes out - at Your word, the moon shines brilliantly upon the earth - You are magnificent! You are awesome! You are marvelous - everything You do is for our good – God, Zeke is good for me and he is good for Your people. Do not allow his missteps to incur Your wrath. Forgive him and thereby grant me a pardon from this hell that I am facing without him, Lord, not just for him but also for everyone on this floor who is fighting for their lives. You know what they are in need of; forgive their sins and blot out their iniquities. I pray this for them, Father, because they cannot pray for themselves, right now. Give them another opportunity to call on You for the grace to remove their trespasses far from them; those undisclosed and soft speaking sins that reside in the place that only You know. Abba, for every time they chose to go against Your will and desire for their lives, whether it is for themselves or for others, forgive them. And not just them, but me as well; if there is any wicked way in me that would hinder my prayer, reveal it so I may surrender it to the fire of Your refining."

Mavet stood outside the door of Pastor Zeke Montgomery and listened to his wife praying for him and everyone. Ever since she has taken up residence in this ward, he has not been able to visit the rooms of all of the patients. It was as if she had arranged some sort of directive, even though he was acquainted with them. He stood seething, as she prayed to her God so fervently for the lives of those she did not even know. She was so sincere in her petitions and cries for their souls. She had been pacing the halls and walking throughout each room in the ward. There had been no place untouched by her invocations.

When she first came into the hospital with her husband lying so still on the gurney, he tried to talk with her. He offered his ear to her because he knew she had to be hurting and was desperate for an empathetic and understanding confidante. She snubbed his attempts, not even acknowledging him when he approached her. At first, he thought it was because she had been so overwrought at the thought of her husband's mortality. Nonetheless, she continued to ignore him and his advances in her direction.

"Lord, show me where to direct my prayers and to what I need to do to combat this spirit that has infiltrated this area."

Mavet began to walk away. Ziva Montgomery opened her eyes and looked toward the doorway.

"There you are," she said, as her eyes locked with Mavet's.

CHAPTER EIGHTEEN

Marissa sat in the window seat looking out into the forested area behind the Palmer's home. She had a funny feeling in the pit of her stomach, as she watched a crow sitting on a branch high up in one of the trees. She noticed there were some chipmunks running in the yard. She knew the crow was looking for the perfect time to swoop in and grab one of the unsuspecting rodents in its talons. She sensed there was something in the atmosphere looking for a spiritual advantage on God's people. She heard the Holy Spirit say, "*Be always on the watch, and pray that you may be able to escape all that is about to happen.*"

 She knew that there were many living their lives without regard to the plans of the enemy. The bible warns that he is walking about seeking whom he may devour. It grieved her that so many were devoured, at the Wisdom Outreach Center, because they were unsuspecting; they refused to watch and pray. Instead, they went about carousing and searching for ways to gain more possessions. She wondered if her father had become one of those people. How else could this evil come so close to their family?

Marissa remembered when she was younger, before her father became a pastor, how they would sit around the table and have bible study. They spent time learning the ways of Christ and praying that He taught them how to stand for the hard right against the easy wrong. She thought back on how her mother would insist that they ask God to give them wisdom and discernment to distinguish between a good thing and a God thing. She encouraged them to seek to stand out and not blend in; and how to be comfortable in their own skin. It was not always easy, but she was glad that she took heed to her mother's words. She did not always make the best decisions, but it was not because she did not try.

She could hear her father praying that nothing would be able to come near their home because God was at the center of everything. Sure, they had hardships and trying times, just like any other family, but it would not be able to destroy them. In every situation, they maintain open lines of communication with each other and God. Unfortunately, that began to change when he became the pastor of the Wisdom

Outreach Center. They still talked with each other, but the conversations were being steered toward what to do to get more people into the church; more so than how they could remain humble, tasked with such an awesome responsibility.

Her mother did more praying than she saw her father doing especially, over the last eighteen months. Her father spent a lot of his days, and nights, making plans and vision boards. Marissa knew this did not sit well with her mother, yet she never complained. She never slacked on her support of her husband. She stood by his side, loving him and entreating God on his behalf. She would tell her and her brother Jaden to pray for their father. The task he had undertaken was a big one and he needed his family to stand with him with both feet on the ground and their hearts turned toward the Lord.

It was not until recently that Marissa knew exactly what her mother meant when she said to stand with her father with both feet on the ground. It was too easy to lose sight of what was important in the world. Too often, things became the focus and people would not be able to grasp their true reality, fully. With this, they would start to seek outside of themselves for material gain to satisfy a thirst that only God could quench. Remaining in the present and seeking the Creator for what their true need was would allow them to walk in truth, on the ground, and not seek a lofty apparition.

As she watched the crow, it became clearer that her commitment to keeping her feet on the ground did not mean that she should not be ever mindful of her surroundings. Another vantage point could always be obtained by seeking God for clarity. This is what she was doing, as she could not push away the sense of impending danger. The chipmunks scampered around, unwittingly drawing dangerous attention to them. Just before the crow began his decent to the ground, Marissa banged on the window, startling the animals and causing them to run to safety.

In that moment, she knew what she was to do. She heard the Lord plainly, "*If the trumpet does not sound a clear call, then who will get ready for battle?*"

Mitrice rode the horse into the wind. She needed to clear her mind and calm her spirit.

The weight of the presence of God was on her in such a way that she could do anything but pray, ever since Pastor Zeke collapsed during morning worship. In fact, she had been in intercessor mode since Analise became deathly ill on her wedding day. She had been sensing something going on in the spirit realm, but she could not quite put her finger on it. Whenever this happened, she just used her spiritual language to take care of the petition. She had no idea what to pray for, but she knew she should be seeking God during this time.

She took a trip out to the Shenandoah Riding Center, and asked for Buttercup, her favorite horse and decided to go for a long ride. As she got further out of the city limits, her spiritual senses heightened. The open air was teeming with activity. The horse became skittish and Mitrice knew she could sense the shift. The winds picked up causing it to feel much cooler than it should, at this time of year. It had been unseasonably cool, anyway, but a sudden briskness was in the air.

Buttercup reared up and whinnied. Mitrice did what she could to try to calm the horse, but she would not settle down. She held tightly to the reins to avoid a throw from the animal, and she spoke into her ear. Her voice was not doing the trick, as it had done in the past. She pranced from side to side, as if she was dodging some assailant. Her nostrils flared, as she snorted and stamped about. Something was troubling the horse and Mitrice did not see anything.

Fear began to creep into Mitrice's spirit. This was a familiar scene and she did not want to see it played out. The memory flooded back and she transported to the riding camp she had attended as a teenager. She could see the horse in front of her, with her best friend on it. Everything was going as it should, until a fox ran out of the woods and started the beast. She yelled out, in an attempt to alert her friend, but the horse bolted and she could hear her friend's terrified screams. She tried to urge her horse to go faster, in an attempt to catch up with her friend and try to calm the steed. However, her horse was not very fast or the most obedient in the camp.

Her friend and the horse were speeding toward the trees at the furthest point of the field. When they reached the forest, the horse reared up, and her friend could not hold on and flew several feet away; she hit a tree with tremendous force. By the time Mitrice could reach her friend, she could tell that things were not good. Her friend lay in a mangled heap, on the ground and the horse was several yards away. She called out, but did not get a response. Blood trickled from her ears and mouth; her eyes were staring blankly toward the ground.

Mitrice yelled for help, but she could not get off her horse. She screamed and cried until one of the camp counselors came riding out to the end of the field. All the while, she remained on her horse, unable to move a muscle. The counselor jumped off his horse and rushed to her friend, then called for help on the walkie-talkie. Within minutes, an ambulance sped toward them and whisked her friend away amidst screeching sirens and flashing lights.

She remembered having to go home, after the incident, because she was unable to get the sight of her friend out of her mind. She sat, in the dark, on the day of the funeral unwilling to believe that she had died right in front of her eyes. She could not fathom how someone her age could be dead; they were too young. Her mother took her to counseling; and the counselors diagnosed her with posttraumatic shock. She could not ride for years without having the scene replay itself in her head. She would have nightmares and awake screaming, sweat glistening from her brow.

It took several years of therapy and much prayer to get back up on a horse, again. Once she turned her life over to Christ, she did not want to have anything terrorizing her. She sought the Lord for peace and freedom from her fears and He had done what she had asked. Riding had become a place of refuge for her once again, until now.

"Get it together, Mitrice!" She scolded herself aloud. "God has not given you a spirit of fear. You will not allow yourself to be consumed by this spirit, again," she continued.

She leaned into the horse, forcing the tension out of her body and spoke into Buttercup's ear, once more. This time she prayed, in the Spirit, and did not use her own anxiety-ridden words. As she heard the words, her body became more at ease. The more she relaxed, the calmer the horse became until she sat still in the middle of the glade.

In that moment, Mitrice could see there was a message. She understood that fear was at the root of what was taking place. People were afraid of missing something or having something taken away and they were willing to do whatever was necessary to secure their possessions. Fears from the past were creeping into the hearts of people causing them to seek alternate means to protect themselves. Because of it, a spirit of destruction had been entertained. Of course, it did not appear as destruction, much like when Adam and Eve had taken of the forbidden fruit; it was subtle, but caustic. It eroded away at their desire for spiritual intimacy with God and offered a substitute in its place.

He showed her just how easy it was to grab hold of the terror by letting her experience it, first hand. She was not to judge those who chose the way of destruction over the path of righteousness. If there were no real commitment to the things of God, fear would win every time. Humanity would seek out fleshly ways to deal with it because it was quicker than seeking Him. She thought back to her attempt to warn her friend of the impending danger.

In that moment, she knew what she was to do. She heard the Lord plainly, "*If the trumpet does not sound a clear call, then who will get ready for battle?"*

Jackson sat in the firehouse, reading his bible. He had been doing more of that since the wedding, and praying more since Sunday's service when Pastor Zeke collapsed. It was too much to see such a strong man cry out as he did before he passed out in his wife's arms. So much was going on, lately, and he needed some grounding force to keep him from cracking under the pressure. He did not grow up in a particularly religious house, but his mother did take them to church from time to time around special holidays.

Whenever his father would come around, his mother sent him to his grandmother's house and she would read bible stories to him and his little sister. She would talk to them about Jesus and the sacrifice He made for them. She told them that no matter what happened or how bleak things seemed that God loved them. As a youth, this comforted him especially when his mother would give into her fits of rage. She would do things to him and his sister that no child should have to face. She would speak railing words filled with venom that fell on their fragile souls like acid on metal. He watched it slowly whittle away at his sister until she threw herself from the roof of the high school.

Still, his grandmother would speak to him about God's love and a person could forgive anything if he or she chose to do so. He remembered asking about making such a hard decision when he was just a kid. Why should he be required to forgive his mother when she was supposed to protect them? His grandmother told him about Jesus' choice to forgive those who beat Him and betrayed Him. He did not do it because it was easy; He did it because it was necessary. She told him that when someone makes the choice to forgive, he or she is choosing God over himself or herself. Whenever that choice was made, God would give them something in return to replace the anger, disappointment and bitterness that came to rest in the bosom of the offended. There was no room for God in a heart harboring things unlike Him. Moreover, just as He chose to let our offenses go, in order to remain close to us, we should choose to forgive others to remain close to Him.

His grandmother's words drove him to church when he found out that he had a brother who lived in Nevis that had never met their father. He knew his father was a native of the West Indian island, but he did not know that he completely turned his back on a family he had there. He had his own issues with his father that stemmed from his mother's abandonment of them whenever he came around, but to know that he left a child and never looked back was more than he could handle. He wanted to hold on to the anger that filled his soul, but his grandmother warned him against it. Anger and fury were like hot coals in the bosom of man, she said. It would only bring destruction to the one who held onto it, while those who offended walked free from its damage.

He and Etmus developed a great relationship, erected on a foundation of truth and freedom. Both men made the decision to forgive their father and their mothers for choosing such a cad. With that, they were able to bond as brothers and friends. His brother had not been a regular at the Wisdom Outreach Center, but he did read his bible from time to time. He shared with him that back in Nevis his mother would talk about God and how important it was to develop a relationship with him. Jackson could tell that his brother was heading back to his roots, now that things were getting out of sorts around him.

Ever since that day at the river's edge when he looked into the eyes of a soulless man, Etmus had been searching for peace. When he came home that night, and they went out for drinks, he could hardly speak. For most of the night they sat, in silence. Jackson prayed, to himself, as he saw the torment that wrapped around his brother. When he could finally verbalize what he witnessed, they both were looking for answers. What happened that created such emptiness in the man? What did they need to do to ensure that did not happen to one of them?

This is what Jackson was searching for in the scriptures. He wanted God to speak to him and tell him what he needed to do to confirm that his soul would remain intact. He felt the pull, within himself, to stand up in the power given to him as a child of the Most High. As he stood praying, in Turner Hall, he knew God wanted him to cry out for those who were lost or losing their way. A sense of urgency took hold of his spirit and he fell to his knees and cried out to God.

In that moment, he knew what he was to do. He heard the Lord plainly, *"If the trumpet does not sound a clear call, then who will get ready for battle?"*

CHAPTER NINETEEN

The scraping on the wall was enough to drive anyone insane let alone someone cooped up in a dark room for countless hours and days. She had no idea how long she had been imprisoned, but she knew it was too long. She kept wondering what was going on behind the large metal doors and beyond the concrete walls that separated her from the rest of the world. She wondered what she must look like and if anyone had hidden cameras in here watching her every move. Were they able to see how unkempt her hair must have been? She had no idea what her clothing looked like, but she was always self-conscious. Notions bombarded her mind that beautiful women of her age scoffed at her.

She wanted to yell out, but her voice eluded her. She wanted to cry, but her fountain of tears had run dry. Perhaps that was a good thing; she did not want to look more ridiculous to the invisible tormenters. She crouched in the corner, hoping to become undetectable to the taunting eyes she felt on her skin. She put her hands over her eyes because she imagined the eyes were just across the room, boring into her soul.

"*Pathetic*," a female voice jabbed.

"*How did you ever survive out in the world?*" another voice echoed.

"*You should be used to the looks of disdain, by now*," a male voice joined in.

The laughter followed and reverberated off the cinder block walls. It started low and then built to a deafening crescendo. She pulled at her hair. She rocked back and forth. She turned to the wall, away from the menacing eyes and the heartless cachinnation. Yet, it continued, relentlessly. There was no escaping the jibes and ridicule. They filled the room. They whispered them in her ears. They shouted out insults; nitpicking at every little thing.

"*Could you not have done something with your hair?*"

"*Have you ever turned down a meal?*"

"*You were never pretty; you should have taken more time with yourself.*"

"*Did you think we would not see you?*"

"Will a man ever really love you?"

"Do you even love yourself?"

She wanted to turn off the incessant chatter, but it droned on and on for what seemed like hours. She wanted to die. Anything would be better than this torture. The voices kept telling her that she would never compare to other women. They reminded her of her inability to have children. They spoke about her husband's infatuation with other women. The words resounded within her like the deep timbre of a bass drum. They repeated themselves like the echo in a cavern. They sped up and slowed down. They swirled and grew larger. She began to repeat them to herself. It was not anything she had not said, during the course of her life. They were not bringing anything new into the equation. This had been her life for as long as she could remember.

"And it will continue to be your life," a familiar voice spoke to her.

"You chose this life for yourself."

"You had options for high couture imaginings, yet you always returned to thrift store thinking."

"You made decisions to insist that someone else's life was always better than your own."

"And you sought me out to agree with you and allow you to pine away for other people's goods. You were never satisfied," the voice that she was accustomed to, spoke again.

She thought about what she heard. She could not deny the words that were being thrown in her face. Even though they spoke against her, she wanted to experience their boldness. They did not fear her or give a second thought to how she would feel hearing them. She thought that they were well dressed and had it all together. It had to be that way; it was always that way. She was never enough and other people always outshined her on so many levels. She did not measure up. *If only I could have had the opportunities that other girls had when I was younger,* she thought to herself.

"And the band plays on," the voice whispered in her ear.

"It was always yours; the power of death and life are in the tongue."

"You wanted to place blame and take the onus off of yourself … so, you did."

"*You wanted to think your life so much worse off than others.*"

"*You wanted to believe other people thought the same way; like their life was the best.*"

"*So, you began to secretly wish their life was your own. You daydreamed about what it would be like if your family was like the neighbors.*"

"*It created a vague bitterness on the inside of you; always thinking others thought they were better than you because that was how you thought.*"

It was true. She knew people were looking at her and her family trying to figure them out. Those she surrounded herself with were always talking about how good they had it. Their constant bragging and flaunting caused her to view her life as subpar. She began to secretly wish their lives would fall apart; not blatant harm, but just a bit of hardship to show them they were no better than she was. She wanted her family to shine like others, but it did not. Why couldn't she have a great relationship like the couple who lived a couple of doors down? Why did things happen that would cause people to gawk and stare in her direction? She wanted the fairytale life that she saw other people living. She deserved it and it made her angry that she did not have it.

"*Just like I said, pathetic*," the voice repeated.

"*It's a vicious cycle; one that was self-created.*"

"*And you grabbed it by the horns and gave up all hope of changing your mind about your situation. So, I gave you what you so desperately wanted … a life of wishing and never having.*"

Jane Doe was thrashing about on her bed. Her heart rate and blood pressure were rising. The doctors ran into the room at the alarms that were sounding on the machines that were keeping her alive. As she was in the throes, of what appeared to be a seizure, the medical staff could hear her bones breaking and tear through her flesh. Her eyes were alternately opening and closing, blinking wildly. The crew could not restrain her due to her fragile bones. The doctor ordered a nurse to inject Dilantin into the vein of her right arm in order to get the seizure under control rapidly.

After several moments, the seizing stopped and Jane Doe lay broken and wounded on the bed. Her eyes were sunken into her head and bruised. Her blood pressure was still dropping, but her heart rate was returning to a normal sinus rhythm. The medical personnel worked to bandage up the open wounds and splint the broken bones. She was too weak to move and they were unsure that her necrotic bones would be able to withstand the weight of a cast. The nurse amped up the morphine drip in an attempt to ease the severity of the pain due to the fractures she had incurred during the seizure.

The staff wrapped the patient in soft splints to keep the broken bones in place, as best as they could. She was going to require extensive plastic surgery, physical and rehabilitative therapy when and if she was to recover. The medical issues affected every bone in her body, including her face, distorted due to the fracturing of the jaw and skull. Jane Doe looked assaulted when they found her body outside of the emergency room door. It was similar to the way they found most of their John and Jane Does, lately.

The doctors and nurses remained in the room until they were certain she was out of the woods with the latest crisis. They administered a drug that would place her in a medically induced coma to give her brain a chance to rest and to stave off future seizures. They did not believe her body would be able to survive another one.

"This woman is in for an uphill battle," one of the doctors spoke.

Her pulse was weak and thready. Her blood pressure was low and heart rate was dangerously low. Her body was bruised and broken; there was no way the staff could rectify that problem. She was in the advanced stages of bone cancer. How she could have been walking around with this much damage to her foundation baffled the doctors. The osteolytic tumors were over activating osteoclastic activity and there just was not enough new bone deposition to replace the weakening boney structures of the body. This was the direct cause of the fractures; her bones were wasting away.

"By the sounds of things, the cancer has spread to her lungs," reported the orthopedic oncologist who was assigned to her case. "We need to run more tests to determine the extent of the damage. We can hear whistling when she breathes, which means her airways are being constricted."

"There is no way she can be moved, at this stage," another member of the team stated. "We can only provide comfort care and hope for the best."

"We may have to amputate her legs due to the instability and the ease at which they fractured during the seizure. The extensive bruising lets us know that there is bleeding from the breaks," the orthopedic surgeon spoke up.

"Again, there is no way we can move her without further risk of fracture or worse."

The team just stood at the door of the room, while the machines beeped and the patient labored to breathe.

"*What do you have to say for yourself?*" A voice questioned.

"*Is there no defense for your abject existence?*"

The woman sighed and hung her head, in defeat. There was nothing she could say...nothing she wanted to say, to defend herself or her life. She was broken with a bruised ego. She had spent the greater part of her life pining over the lives other people lived. As long as she remembered, she was never satisfied with her life and the things she possessed. It was never enough; she was never enough. She existed to watch others live the life of her dreams. She would spend hours fantasizing about what it would be like to be this person or that person. She wondered what she would do if she didn't have to be concerned about her diet - what it would be like to have a spouse who loved her with an all-consuming passion – what it would be like to worry about her children – what it would be like to have her siblings and parents be close-knit. If only...

"*Don't you ever get tired of hoping and wishing for someone else's life?*"

"*How do you deal with the secret misery and your closet longing?*"

She had no answers for the voices, in her head. All she could muster was a dejected breath. The more they taunted, the more she realized how pitiable her miserable life had become. She had no defense. She did want what other people had. Why couldn't she have just a tiny morsel of happiness for herself? Why couldn't her marriage be enviable? Why couldn't she have the body of a super model? Why couldn't her womb be fertile? Why couldn't she be the pastor's wife?

CHAPTER TWENTY

Mavet walked away from Ziva Montgomery's stare. As much as he wanted her out of the picture, he was not ready to deal with her, just yet. He knew he would not be able to contend with her when she was this amped up by prayer and meditation. He was no fool. There would be a better opportunity; he was sure of it. In the meantime, he needed to go down to see what was going on with one the Jane Doe down the hall. He noticed the doctors and nurses running into her room. As he approached the window looking into her room, he smiled.

The doctors were taking every conceivable measure to preserve this woman's life. In the face of death, they refused to let her go without a fight. However, what could they really do for her? She was in the end stages of bone cancer, which had spread to her lungs. Any healthy bone wasted away or pushed to its limits by the tumors that ravaged her body. Her breathing was labored and her vital organs were overworked. It would not be long before she would not be able to hold on and her body would shut down.

There was nothing more he could do here, so he decided to go take care of other pressing matters. He would not walk back past Zeke's room on the off chance that Ziva would be looking for him. He headed toward the back stairwell, opened the door and began his descent to the main level of the hospital. He traversed the corridor as he headed toward the lobby and out into the open air. The temperatures had dropped since he arrived and he pulled his shirt collar up. He walked into the street and headed for the parking lot.

It was late afternoon and he knew where he would find Ghrelin. He would be with Galia and Phineas' boy, Axel. They needed to have a long discussion about how he was handling his assignments. There was no reason for the lackadaisical manner in which he was going about his job. He could not understand why he invested so much time into those whom he interacted with; he was not supposed to implant himself into their lives, as he had done. He trained to remain aloof and distant; appear involved without real commitment. Yet, this was not the case. He had spent two decades with the Mitchell girl and now it looked like he was settling in for the long haul with Axel. This was not acceptable. In fact, it was downright unprofessional.

Ghrelin was acting like an amateur; a wet nosed novice. He appeared to need those to whom he was assigned more than he made them need him. He was to build a foundation of hunger that was to grow to insatiable heights. Their appetites were to swell and engorge until they became self-thriving forces; this is when he was supposed to introduce them to Mavet. But, this was not happening. He was keeping them for himself; as if they were satisfying some need in him. He was weak and that was not good for this call of duty. He needed reprimanding.

Mavet stood outside of the Fitzhugh's house watching Ghrelin and Axel interact with each other. Axel sprawled out on the sofa playing video games, drinking a beverage. Mavet moved in to get a closer look and to listen to their conversation.

"You will need to busy yourself with something, Axel, or your parents are going to keep harassing you to get a job," Ghrelin was saying.

"I have been doing things, man. I joined the fitness center and I have been filling out applications, online. They act as if I am just sitting around, all of the time. I am just not doing what they want, so they think I'm doing nothing."

"They think you should be working toward something."

"Yeah, they want me to live my life their way. My mom told me this morning, that I should be taking classes or looking for an internship. I told her I do not have time for that, right now."

In fact, his parents were angling for him to get more involved in the church. When he was younger, they thought he was going to be a part of the mission team, full time. He seemed to enjoy the outreach activities and even mentioned going on an assignment to one of the orphanages that the church sponsored in Guatemala. His father tried to put him on the fast track to becoming a youth leader for the teen missionary group in the church they attended, at the time. Axel thought it was a good idea, at first. He contemplated majoring in

International Relations so he could better serve others. However, he found other things to occupy his time and douse the flame of ambition. His parents thought he was going and would be a great foreign affairs diplomat, but steer it into the direction of ministry.

The more his mother and father pushed, the less and less he pushed himself. He made the choice not to declare a major in college, to take the pressure off him. He would not join any ministry at the Wisdom Outreach Center; instead, he busied himself with menial tasks. He linked up with groups that had nothing to do with helping others to keep his parents mouths shut about him staying busy. The phone rang. Axel got up, walked into the kitchen, and picked up the receiver.

Ghrelin looked up and saw Mavet standing outside. He motioned for him to join him on the lawn. He got up and headed toward him. He did not have a good feeling about an encounter. He knew that Mavet was not pleased with the way he was handling his assignment, but he was doing what he thought best. He thought he could do a better job, if he worked it alone. Why did he need to hand off things to Mavet?

"Because that is what you are directed to do, Ghrelin." Mavet answered.

"You know there was nothing set in stone, when I took these assignments," Ghrelin argued.

"You are not authorized to take matters into your own hands."

"Why, Mavet? So you can get all the credit and I get nothing?"

"This is not about credit for either one of us and you know that, you simpleton! You have been allowed to jaunt about making friends and prolonging the inevitable. We are not here to form longstanding bonds with these people – what do you think has been happening while you have been gallivanting about? Plans are being made to replace you."

The skies grew darker, as they walked and talked. The winds picked up and lightening flashed. Ghrelin looked back at the Fitzhugh house and noticed there was an amber glow coming from the inside of it. He turned to go back, but Mavet stood in his way. He attempted to go around him; however, he was unable to move quickly enough. A dense fog began to roll in and permeate the walls of the house

"The time has come, Ghrelin. Your services are no longer needed, in this town. You failed your assignment and there are consequences to your inadequacy. You chose yourself over the goal of the mission and I am here to deliver the judgment," Mavet seemed to grow in stature and presence.

Ghrelin could not believe this was happening without thought for innocent bystanders. Wasn't there some clause about revealing their true nature? He was not afraid. He had seen a reassignment in the past.

"Get on with it!" Ghrelin shouted over the tempest.

Several small tornadoes spawned from the storm; and in them, were the members of the council assigned to cases that were much graver than a mere reassignment. They sat in silence as they waited to hand down the sentence. Afterward, they would vote and exact punishment. Ghrelin only knew this from hearsay, but those called into question by this group were never heard from again. Their eyes glowed and an acrid smoke escaped their partly closed lips. Their stares held him fast in his place. He recognized no mercy; there was only judgment. Fear rose from his belly and spilled out onto the ground; it wrapped around his feet, moved up to his ankles, and shackled him to the earth.

"Not so bumptious now, are you Ghrelin?" Mavet walked around him, careful not to step in the evidence of fear on the ground. "You are a disgrace to the confederation. You have consistently overstepped your authority and been delinquent in relinquishing those in your care into the next phase of the assignment. Instead, you have coddled them and ingrained yourself into their lives making it necessary to extricate you from your duties."

"You have created a situation that was not intended," one of the council spoke to Ghrelin. "Because of your own overwhelming need for more you have committed an egregious malefaction."

Ghrelin knew what his crime was and he had no mitigation for it. When he received the task of Analise Mitchell, he understood that he would be turning her over to Mavet for more training and refining. It was nothing set in stone, but the assignment was picture perfect for the path of destruction. She was young and impressionable. She needed a little hand holding, in the beginning, but it became evident that she would be ready for the big leagues very early on. Her will was much stronger than Ghrelin's and he soon became her support team, rather than the leader. He was okay with the role he played in her life. He felt needed and important when he was in her company.

"She was exploiting you and your ability to make her feel good," Mavet spat out. "After a while you were not molding her, she was molding you to fit her needs. And by the time you realized what was going on, it was too late; and you were content being her patsy."

"What did you do to her at the wedding?" Ghrelin could not resist the question. He knew Mavet was involved.

"I reached in and touched her where her heart was; in her gut; and took what she nurtured for me. You wanted it for yourself, but it was never yours to begin with, Ghrelin. She outgrew you. She was ready for me and you withheld her from me."

"So you kidnapped her?" Ghrelin spoke, softly.

A vicious and grating laughter erupted from Mavet, filling the air around them. He despised sniveling imps like Ghrelin. Their need to be more, than created for, caused them to become impotent. They allowed themselves to swell to great and lofty heights on puffs of air spouted by those they were supposed to lord over. It was a human trait that some of the agents took on. They held on to vain imaginings, much like humankind, that the destiny of another could be theirs if they simply aspired to have it.

"You are an imbecile, Ghrelin! I could not kidnap what was never yours to begin with. Do you not see that? Vicarious living is not living; it is coveting and that is a trait for humans. The dissatisfaction that comes with not accepting the greatness that has been placed on the inside of you comes from ungrateful people, not us!" Mavet continued to circle around Ghrelin.

"Let's move on," one of the council members spoke.

"Ghrelin, you are being charged with treason and defection. Your actions, as well as your lack of action, speak volumes and there is no need to bring forth witnesses."

"We, the council, find you guilty as charged," the entire group spoke in unison.

In that moment, Mavet stood face to face with Ghrelin. He could smell the fear emanating from his body. He smiled, as he looked into the condemned imp's eyes.

"I have been waiting to do this for a long time," Mavet breathed.

In that moment, Mavet moved closer to Ghrelin and reached one hand behind his head, the other positioned in front of his belly. A sharp talon appeared at the ends of each of his fingers. In one swift motion, he ripped into his body and a searing pain made its way to Ghrelin's core. A demented laugh escaped his lips as his essence left him. In a puff of smoke, he was gone.

The swirling winds and rolling fog dissipated, leaving the atmosphere charged but settled. The council had returned to their rightful place and Mavet straightened himself as he wiped what remained of Ghrelin from his hands. He looked over to the Fitzhugh house to confirm his presence was no longer apparent before heading back to the hospital. He had to check on one thing before he returned, later that evening. Galia would be ready for him after she arrives home to find her son lying dead on the kitchen floor.

Evan and Katrice Mitchell kept vigil at their daughter's bedside since that fateful day. They resisted the urge to pass judgment on Miles for not coming to visit her once since she was brought into the hospital. Evan could not imagine what must be going through his mind after seeing his fiancé lying on the floor as blood poured from her rectum, staining her diamond white bridal gown to a crimson red.

There were touch and go moments, as the medical staff fought to stave out one deadly infection after another, as fecal matter poured into her body unchecked. Analise battled high fevers and convulsions. Her kidneys were working overtime in an attempt to fill her body with fluids to wash the poison from her system. Because of this, an incredible amount of bloating took place, until her kidneys stopped working. A dialysis machine was now doing the work to flush her severely toxic system.

The machines began to screech and alarms began to sound. The wearied couple stood back as the staff rushed to the room. This had become a routine event, since the day she arrived here from Galena. Their daughter was a fighter and never succumbed to the welcoming hands of death. They pushed medicine into the intravenous port, as they had done so many times during her stay. This time seemed different. As Evan and Katrice stared on, Analise Mitchell went into septic shock. The intensive care nurse opened her line, flooding her with fluids and large amounts of antibiotics, as directed by the doctor. Her blood pressure began dropping at an alarming rate and the staff asked her parents to leave the room.

Evan took his wife by the hand and escorted her into the hallway, as the nurse closed the curtain. Tears fell freely down their faces. They feared the worst. They could hear the staff talking just beyond the enclosure. They worked diligently to save their daughter's life, but to no avail.

"Time of death, five o'clock," the doctor called.

The curtain opened and one of the staff doctors walked out into the hall.

"We are sorry. We did everything we could to save her, but her body was just too weak. The inflammation caused by sepsis created microscopic blood clots, which blocked vital nutrients to her main organs. Your daughter has expired."

"Nooooo!" The exclamation erupted from the opposite end of the hall. Miles Kirkpatrick, escorted by Jarhys Houston, fell to the floor.

CHAPTER TWENTY-ONE

When Ziva recognized Mavet standing in the doorway, she immediately changed her course of intercession and began to pray against destruction and its cohorts, terror and anguish. She could hear grief as it walked the halls of the intensive care unit of Mercy Medical Center. Analise Mitchell had died just before her fiancé could make amends for his absence. She heard her parents begin to blame him for his cowardice and refused him access into her room. The pleading was heart wrenching but it did not move the couple. Their anguish over the death of their daughter was much stronger than his penitent sorrow for not being by her side. She could feel the turmoil rise to extraordinary heights, affecting the other patients.

Alarms sounded throughout the floor, but Ziva refused to allow it entrance into her husband's room. She pleaded the blood of Jesus with confidence and fervor. She called on the name of the Lord and petitioned His ministering angels to take up residence in the four corners of his room. She asked them to encamp around his bed and surround his head. She placed her hands on his sternum and cried out for God to heal the inflammation and bring him back to her. The two of them would best handle this situation. She was not leaving room for sudden destruction to infiltrate their lives.

"Not on my watch!" Ziva called out to the evil spirit.

She walked out of the room and walked the halls, praying in the Spirit. She went over to Miles and put her hands on his forehead. She commanded anguish, guilt and shame to expel from his life. She called out trauma and grief, in the name of Jesus. Jarhys Houston had stepped aside to allow the First Lady access to his friend who knelt, dejectedly, in the halls. He closed his eyes hoping his life would not hinder his friend from his deliverance. He quietly asked God to forgive his transgressions and place him on the straight and narrow.

The floor began to tremble as Ziva went to war for the people of the Wisdom Outreach Center. The doctors and nurses scurried from room to room trying to put out the fires of destruction that had been set. All the patients were going into crisis at the same time. There was not enough staff to cover the emergencies. A nurse ran to the desk and called a hospital wide code blue; this would have other doctors rushing to their aid. She ran to Jane Doe, diagnosed with the end stages of bone cancer. Her heart monitor was beeping incessantly. Pulmonary edema had set in and the pressure was squeezing her heart muscle. Immediately, a syringe entered her body and the fluid rushed out, relieving the pressure.

John Doe with the necrotizing kidney disease was in distress, as was the Jane Doe with severe endocarditis. Other patients were flatlining when the doorway to the stairwell opened and the elevator bells sounded. Doctors flooded the ward and went into any room unoccupied by staff. They performed life-saving measures on each person at a hurried pace. There was no time to waste. No one had seen this happen before and staff had no time to ponder the cause of such chaos. They had to get the situation under control and fast!

After Ziva left Miles, she ran down the hall to the Mitchells. She could not allow an unforgiving spirit to rest in their bosoms. She spoke against the nasty bile of bitterness that sought to take up root in their lives. She commanded un-forgiveness to flee from them, never to return. She prayed for their souls and beseeched God to give them the strength to stand in their choice to forgive. She implored Him to place an immovable peace deep with their hearts because they were vital to the kingdom of God. She spoke to the terror that sought to overtake Katrice. She cried out against the anguish that wanted assess to Evan.

"You will have no place, in their lives, in the name of Jesus," Ziva commanded, forcefully.

She encouraged them to pray for each other and bar the enemy from coming into their lives to wreak havoc. She took their hands and placed them into the other, "Pray for your wife, Evan. Katrice, pray for your husband."

Ziva could hear her husband coughing, violently, in his room. She turned to head back to his room and bumped into one of the head doctors of the hospital. He grabbed her by the hand and ordered her to help in the rooms. He understood that she was off duty, but they needed her to help during this crisis.

Mavet stood just outside of the doorway leading to the stairwell and nodded toward the doctor.

The concrete walls shook, violently. The foundation of the structure rose and fell as the quake rumbled on. The sound of rattling chains and tormented screams filled the halls. A fire had broken out, as one of the candles overturned and landed on the makeshift cot in one of the rooms. The occupants' terrified screeches cascaded throughout the building, as they found their voices within their terrorized throats.

One voice rose above the din. He was not crying out in pain or fear. He was calling out to the imprisoned souls and telling them to repent. Billows of smoke began to fill the halls and rooms. Coughs filled the air, as everyone began to gasp for breath. The voice continued to entreat them to ask for forgiveness.

"We have allowed our selfish ambitions to occupy the space that should have been set aside for God," he spoke. "This is why we are here, bound by the lusts of our own flesh. These are the words that have been engraved on the stones that hold us hostage. Look deep inside and know what you have hoisted as an idol in your life. Mine was greed. I pulled and pulled seeking to gain more without fully giving what God intended. I wanted to receive more than I gave. Sure, it looked like I was generous, when in fact I had a secret motive. My acts of charity were false and came from an unclean place."

Another voice rose above the clamoring chains. "I allowed my anger to get the best of me. I blamed and punished others, but it was really me. My feeling of inadequacy ran roughshod and unchecked. My anger should have been reigned in; instead, I gave it free course to spill out and onto those around me. I am sorry, God for letting my rage take precedence over Your peace."

The fire that had broken out in one of the rooms consumed everything within and spilled out into the halls. The shaking grew more intense and the chains on the two men who had cried out to God instead of fear were broken. The doors to their cell flung open and they ran out into the corridor trying to help the others held captive. The doors held fast, and they would not budge. The occupants begged for rescue, but refused to pray for themselves.

"Pray people," the two men screamed.

The sound of a rushing train filled the air as hordes of guards ran into the halls. Some carried what looked like Billy clubs in their hands and began banging on the closed doors. Others ran toward the two men seeking to apprehend them and return them to their cells. The men ran in the opposite direction still calling for the people to pray and ask God to forgive them. Just before the guards could ensnare them, an apparition that took the form of a very large hand grabbed them up and out of the fray.

Pastor Zeke Montgomery coughed and coughed, as he fought to come out from under the sedation that held his body to the bed. His eyes were open, but he still could not move on his own. A nurse ran into the room as she noticed him fighting and choking. She stopped the machine that had been delivering a steady dose of the sedative to him, and then closed off the intravenous line that was going into his arm.

Within minutes, his eyes were able to focus and he could exercise the use of his limbs. The nurse encouraged him to take his time, since they had administered drugs to allow his body a chance to fight the infection in his chest. He took heed of the advice, and remained steady on the bed. He could sense the encampment around his room. He knew he was safe. He closed his eyes and rested.

John Doe number two opened his eyes and looked around the room. He felt drained and his limbs were heavy with exhaustion. He could hear the machines and feel the wires that attached to his body. His head was throbbing and he experienced a crushing pain on his left side, just under his heart. He slowly breathed in and out, forbidding himself to give in to the pain or the fear. As he calmed down, the pain began to subside. His eyes began to focus as he tried to make sense of what was going on. Why was he in this hospital room and not at the river's edge apprehending the suspect?

Gavin Palmer did not like feeling dazed and confused. The last thing he remembered was blinking through debris and trying to focus his eyes on a man standing close to the water of the Mississippi River. He recalled hearing the cars racing overhead on the bridge of US Highway 20. He had been investigating a mysterious call that had come into the station house requesting that he come to the scene alone. He knew that Gray Jenkins and Etmus Sadiyo were at the top of the trail searching for anything they may have missed in the investigation of the disappearance of Maddock Hamilton.

"Hello," Gavin called out, weakly.

A nurse came into the room and then ran back out to get one of the doctors. She provided a brief explanation of Gavin's case, recapping how he had been in a coma since arrival. She told the attending that the patient had extensive damage to his liver with a severely distorted face; but that seemed to have remedied. They checked and rechecked his vitals. They peered into his eyes and stated there was no sign of the severe jaundice that plagued him from the beginning of his stay. His skin had returned to its natural pallor and his blood pressure was normal.

Gavin looked over at the empty seat by the window. He wondered why neither Nora nor Katriel seemed to have been sitting with him.

He thought they had abandoned him and left him to die in this hospital alone. He had treated them poorly, and he deserved any mistreatment that came his way. They were probably relieved that he was lying here, near death. He imagined that they were hoping for his demise thereby releasing them from the hell that had become their lives, because of him.

"No one knew who you were so we could not reach out to anyone," the nurse said to him when she realized that he was looking at the chair.

"I did not have any identification on me, when I was brought in?" Gavin questioned, in a raspy tone.

"No sir. In fact, when you arrived to the ward, they advised that you had been left at the emergency room doors. There was no one to tell us who you were or what happened to you," she answered.

Gavin felt relief flood through him. His wife and daughter had no idea that he as in the hospital fighting for his life. They probably thought he had ventured off on one of his outings and would return home in the usual manner drunk and belligerent. On the other hand, they were thinking that he had abandoned them as he so often threatened. He remembered the countless times that he taunted them with words of his departure. He railed about going off and finding a family who appreciated him and his sacrifice. Tears of regret spilled out of his eyes.

"We will have to perform some blood work on you, sir," the doctor was speaking.

"My name is Gavin Palmer. I am the chief of police in Galena, Illinois. My wife works at Mercy Medical Center as a cardiologist on the pediatric unit," he offered.

"Dr. Nora Palmer is your wife?" The nurse asked.

"Yes, do you know her?"

"Sir, you are in Mercy Medical Center," the doctor added.

Gavin began to be concerned about the staff getting involved in their personal lives. He knew his status and that of his wife; and, he did not want to cause trouble for her. He wondered if he had contracted full-blown AIDS and that was the cause of his illness. He realized that he could not afford to remain silent on this point.

"I am sure you are aware that I am HIV positive, by now. Have I developed a complication of that?" He was embarrassed and fought against the anger that was rising in his belly.

"You have liver disease, Mr. Palmer. It could have occurred for a number of reasons. Is your wife aware that you are infected with the virus?"

"Yes, she has been tested," Gavin replied, as shame replaced anger.

"Well, that is what is important, at this juncture. We will get her on the phone and let her know you are here."

"Thank you," Gavin stated.

Ziva remained prayerful as she did what was necessary for the patient experiencing a crisis. She assisted the doctor and administered the appropriate medication in order to abate the near death experience. The woman looked vaguely familiar as she stood over her bleeding wounds. She wrapped them in gauze, as gently as she could, and stared into her face. She could sense this woman was in turmoil. Her face was contorted due to the fractures, but there was something else written all over it. She was in a much more critical battle, Ziva discerned. There was so much more going on underneath the surface. She leaned in and whispered in her ear. "God loves you."

The First Lady realized the power that left her body when she spoke those words. It was for this Jane Doe, it was for all of the Jane Does and the critically ill people, both physically and spiritually. They sounded so simple to the casual observer, but those words carried life in them for all who chose to live by them. "God loves you," she whispered, again.

The woman opened her eyes and stared, sadly, into Ziva's face. She could not speak but there were volumes communicated. Tears rolled down the face of both women, one because of despondency and the other due to empathy.

"Maren, it's Ziva," the First Lady spoke. "What has happened that has gotten you to this place of utter misery?" the tears dropped onto the broken face of her husband's administrative assistant.

"I can't," the words whistled through slightly parted lips.

"Sweetheart, you have so much more than what you believe. Whatever your situation, God's love has the amazing strength to pick you up and carry you through it."

Maren turned her head away from Ziva. It was more than she could entertain in this moment. Why did she have to wake up and see the face of the woman whose life she so desperately wanted? This was proof that God's love did not extend to her or he would not have had her be the first thing she saw when she opened her eyes. She hated her life and wanted it to be over.

Ziva walked out of the room and over to the nurse's station and picked up the phone. She dialed a number and held the receiver to her ear, waiting for someone to answer the ring.

"Adley, it is Ziva. Maren is here at Mercy Medical Center. She is in bad shape and she needs you here with her. She needs your support."

Ziva hung up the phone and headed for her husband's room. She needed to see his handsome face.

CHAPTER TWENTY-TWO

Pastor Zeke was glad to be back in the house of God. He had survived an ordeal that others did not overcome. There were members of the Wisdom Outreach Center who lost life, who would forever be missed. He prayed that the incredible lesson in the midst of destruction not be overlooked by any who were beholden to it. He never went as far as to say they had sold their souls to the devil, but they sought out a means to an end that cost them dearly. A debt was owed and those who tasted of the forbidden delicacies of the flesh had to pay the piper. No one was left unscathed by the self-directed paths they had chosen.

Ziva stood at the podium to address the congregation, as was her custom. Zeke was a blessed man and he would never let that bit of knowledge elude him, again. He had so much more than the average person was, and God has seen fit to grace him with more life. He was not referring to his physical existence, although he will be forever grateful to God for sparing him; he was speaking of his spiritual life. He had been reborn the day he woke up in that hospital room; he was revived. This revival spirit roamed throughout the aisle of the Wisdom Outreach Center. People were learning to live and understand what it meant to be alive. There were handicaps and permanent scars for some that proved as constant reminders of God's providence.

"Good morning, children of God," Ziva spoke. "How many of you are glad to see your pastor back in the building?"

A thunderous applause erupted in the sanctuary. The congregation stood and cheered for their man of God.

"Welcome back, pastor!"

"We sure did miss you!"

"What a blessing to see you!"

Ziva looked back at Zeke. What a journey they had endured these past few weeks. It was something to be thankful for, but she did not want to face the thought of losing her husband again. Their family was back on track, praying and studying the bible together. Jaden was an awesome teacher and Marissa was a powerful intercessor; she used her gift of discernment to direct her prayers and make them more effective.

"God has a mighty work for him to do and He made sure that he returned to his sheep. In his weakness, the Lord's strength is made evident."

Zeke stood to his feet and joined his wife. He took her by the hand and kissed her gently on the lips. He knew how blessed he was and how God spared his life when judgment should have been his recompense. He was a changed man and he had his wife to thank for that. She heeded the call of the Spirit to turn her plate down and pray for him and the entire Wisdom Outreach Center. She bombarded heaven and took on the enemy's hosts to command them to release their hold on God's people. It was his turn to do his part to commit to the assignment as shepherd to the flock that God gave him.

"Church, we are living in perilous days," Zeke began.

"True dat, Passah!" A lone voice yelled out from the back of the sanctuary. The people laughed at the sound, but applauded the sentiment.

"The bible tells us that the enemy walks about, like a roaring lion, seeking whom he may devour. Many of us have made ourselves a scrumptious meal for him. We have seasoned our lives with the herbs of the flesh and roasted in the fires of self-direction. We have to turn the spotlight inward and see if there is any wicked way in us. When I speak of wickedness, I mean any things, thoughts or attitudes that we twist to fit our own agenda. Are there any surreptitious ambitions, concealed emotions or implicit words that we feel the need to justify in order for us to continue in them? Are we secretly wicked? I will go ahead and ask the question, are we overtly wicked?"

Ziva took her seat. She knew that God had something to say to His people and the order of service changed. The offering was going to wait.

"When we think of wickedness, today, we are thinking about murder or Satan worship. But, what is God's meaning of the word? Let's talk about design and functionality. I know it may sound like I am getting off topic, but stay with me. If I go into a house and see a plate on the table, I am told that it is designed to put food on it; some potatoes, carrots, steak and salad

– its function is to hold food. But, if I take that same plate and throw it across the room and it breaks into hundreds of pieces, I have destroyed the functionality or design of the plate; what it was created to do. My action of breaking the plate or destroying it is an act of 'RA' or wickedness."

Pastor Zeke walked around the rostrum and stood on the edge of the pulpit. He looked out into the congregation and tears began to well up in his eyes.

"Church, I became guilty of wickedness when I twisted God's intention for this ministry by making it about numbers. I did what David did in the first book of Chronicles chapter twenty-one, I allowed Satan to incite me to number the people. Likewise, by doing so, I turned the design of this church into something that God did not advise. How many of us have taken a pure purpose or vision and manipulated and twisted it into something that best suits us and not its original intent? We manipulate our relationships so they fit what we want instead of God's original intent. We use our anger to hurt people rather than to empower people to change. When Jesus overthrew the table of the money changers, he wanted them to see the error of their ways and how they had taken God's law and manipulated it for their gain."

The church was quiet as they listened to the pastor make his confession. Many of them thought about how they broke from God's intention for the things and people. Gavin thought about how he used his anger to manipulate and terrorize his family. He bowed his head and Nora took his hand. She had forgiven him and told him as much. Katriel had noticed a change in her father; he was not the same man that left their home all those weeks ago.

In the silence, Marissa could hear the Lord urging her to speak. She stood up and said what she heard in her spirit.

"If My people, who are called by My name, will humble themselves and pray and seek My face and turn from their wicked ways, then I will hear from heaven, and I will forgive their sin and will heal their land." Tears fell from her face, as she repeated the words. "You will need to turn your backs on the ways you have made for yourselves. You will need to turn away from distorting My word to make it fit your agenda. You will need to turn away from your frivolous emotions and your selfish desires. You will need to turn away from reacting out of the lusts of your flesh and justifying it with bible words. Seek Me for direction, any other way is wicked."

Mitrice Reynolds felt God giving her more on what was being said, she stood up.

"I have not given you a spirit of fear; but of power and love and a sound mind. Many of you are walking around afraid of losing something or afraid of not gaining an advantage. I want you to know that you have the power to overthrow the wicked one and to cast down the thoughts that he comes to put into your mind. I will keep you in perfect peace, if you keep your mind on Me, saith the Lord. Do not look to the left or to the right, I am Love and I will give you the power to exhibit love in every situation. Just seek My face and not your own agenda."

"Do not allow un-forgiveness to take root in your heart, saith God," Jackson Harris was speaking. "The enemy will produce many reasons to take and hold on to offenses. I say, let them go! Nothing should take up space in your spirit or your heart that will not leave room for Me. Forgive because I forgive. Forgive because it pushes out wicked desires and thoughts. Forgive because it overshadows fear. Forgive because the evil one is looking for an opening and bitterness leaves a deep cavernous hole, opportunity for destruction. Un-forgiveness is like hot coals in the bosom of man. Repent and forgive. Forgive others and forgive yourself."

Adley Dane cried out, in the sanctuary. "Oh God, forgive me and help me to forgive myself!" He jumped up from his seat and ran to the front of the church. "Oh, God, I am sorry! O God, help me! Help me! Help me!" His tormented screams echoed throughout the building.

Pastor Zeke came off the podium and quickly walked over to Adley. He had sprawled himself across the altar and wept without regard to the onlookers. Zeke put his arms around him and he buried his head into his chest.

"Why did I listen to her?" He cried. "Why did I not try to convince her that my love would help her through it all? Instead, my love turned wicked and I justified my actions. I killed my wife, Pastor. I listened to her tell me that her life was not worth living in the condition that she was in. She didn't want to live being mangled and disfigured and in excruciating pain. She wanted to be out of her misery. So, I justified putting the pillow over her face until she stopped breathing, by saying I was doing it out of love." He let out a most pitiable bellow.

Jackson walked up to the front of the church and embraced Adley. "God said, forgive yourself for your actions and forgive her for asking you to do it."

Ziva walked down from the podium and over to Adley. "Do not torture yourself, Adley. Maren was not dead when you left the room."

"What?"

"You left the room, thinking she was dead, but she was not."

"But she is dead, First Lady," he cried.

"Yes, Adley, she is dead – she died when the bone cancer spread to her lungs and she could no longer breathe. You did not kill your wife."

"God is saying to forgive yourself because you took action, not because your actions caused her death. He said forgive yourself for giving up on Him and giving in to your wife."

"Church, we need to pray and pray some more," Pastor Zeke stated. "The enemy has set his sights on the Wisdom Outreach Center and we need to be fortified against his attack. We weathered one onslaught, and encountered some casualties. I am sensing in my spirit that this is not the last of it. We need to pray."

The council convened after the major disruption and the loss of souls. The walls were in shambles and the chains of many had been broken. The guards were able to secure the scant few, but not before others had escaped. Mavet stood in the center of the room facing a jury of his peers. He knew they were looking to place blame and he was the likely culprit. It was his responsibility to take care of the parishioners of the Wisdom Outreach Center. He was to keep them so wrapped up that they did not see what was happening.

He was to blind them to their power and ability to change the face of Galena. The council had plans for the agricultural area. They wanted to set up a stronghold, which was to be the hub of a major takeover of the entire Midwestern region. The Wisdom Outreach Center started out the spiritual powerhouse God intended and they could not have them succeed. They sent Mavet to distract the people and get them off of their assignment. He had been doing a good job, until lately. He lost control and now they were in the middle of a crisis. The people took hold of the fact that God's Son had paid the price for their sins and that they did not have to accept the charge. When they cried out to God for forgiveness, the council lost their right to hold them.

Kaveid stood up from behind the long table. His sulfuric breath filled the air. He looked intently at Mavet, with his yellow eyes. He was silent for a few moments, before he spoke.

"You disappoint us, Mavet," his gravelly voice came forth. "We had such high hopes in you and your ability to produce for us."

"It was that woman..." Mavet began.

"A woman, Mavet?" Kaveid asked.

"Yes, Ziva Montgomery has been a real nuisance."

Kaveid walked around the table to stand in front of Mavet. He did not speak; he just stared at Mavet. The rest of the council remained silent, as well. Mavet did not speak; he awaited the verdict. He did not think they would banish him, or worse, he knew he was powerful and well capable of handling his job. This was a minor setback in his eyes - something to remedy by removing the obstacle. He knew what he had to do.

"Mavet, it seems as if this woman is more of a match than you anticipated," Kaveid breathed.

"I did not believe she would be such a force," Mavet confessed.

"So, you did not do your homework on this woman, the First Lady of the church?" Kaveid questioned. "You will need some assistance with her, it seems."

Mavet thought about the statement. He did not want to admit that he had met his match with Ziva Montgomery. Nothing he has done has worked with her. He could not find a crack big enough to slip into; she would not even entertain his conversations. She seemed an impenetrable force. He tried everything. He approached her when she was disappointed, sad and angry. She always quickly closed the gaps with prayer and fasting.

"I will go with you and together we can push her until she breaks," Kaveid spoke as he walked back to his seat.

"In the meantime, we will reconvene on the issue of your failures, thus far; and how much they have cost us. We have lost ground and that has to be addressed, Mavet."

CHAPTER TWENTY-THREE

The woman laid on the floor after the fire broke out in her room on the fateful day that the earth moved. She was unable to escape the hellish nightmare unscathed. She suffered burns to her face and hands, as well as inhaling large amounts of smoke. She thought how irresponsible it had been for those in charge to leave candles so close to a heap of cloth. Had she not been chained, perhaps she would have been able to move it to the opposite side where nothing would be fodder for the flame had the candle turned over. She attributed her life to her quick thinking to hover close to the cold cement blocks across from the mat. The flames licked at her skin, but did not consume her. She wondered if anyone else had thought to do the same thing; or if the rest thought to use their cot to shield them from the billowing smoke.

It did not matter, she thought. She was on the mend and she had no one to thank for it, but herself. She heard the man, who mysteriously found his voice, yelling for everyone to repent and ask God for forgiveness for the way they had lived their lives. She had nothing to apologize for or to seek redemption from, in her life. She made good, solid decisions that did not require any assistance from an outside source. She had the wherewithal to choose well and her family benefited well from those choices. She did not know what was going on, at this particular juncture of her life; but she felt confident that she would discover a way to make it work to her advantage. She would learn to make the most of this situation until she could get back to her husband and kids.

"*Your pride will be the death of you*," a voice echoed, in the room.

"*Pride comes before destruction*," another spoke out.

"*You are the only left from the group you belonged to; what do you have to say about that?*"

"*You don't have an idea what you are dealing with; and you never will.*"

"*They were smarter than you were and found a way out.*"

She had learned to tune out the voices, just as she had done when she was younger. She would not allow them to cause her to go back to that time in her life when she felt insignificant. She would not go back into that closet where her uncle would take her control away. He would not let her speak or make decisions. She tried to tell him that if he would just give her the chance that maybe she could love him, in return. He would not listen to her. He told her that she did not know what she was talking about; had no idea about the things of the world or of love. He did not want her to speak, just lie still until he was finished. He repeated in her ear, as he assaulted her young body, "*You are just a dumb female. You don't know anything and you never will. You don't have anything to say that anyone wants to hear.*"

She remembered shrinking on the inside as his words echoed in her soul. As she got older and she immersed herself in books, she found her power. She knew she was intelligent and that she would be able to use her smarts to get anything she wanted. She was able to outwit her uncle and he never took her to the closet, again. She would be able to use her intelligence to figure out what to do to be free of the chains that held her fastened to the ground. She fought against the notion that she would be locked away, becoming insignificant once more. She rose up, within herself, and refused to consider that she was less than what she believed.

"*I have grown weary of your haughtiness*," a familiar voice spoke.

The chains broke and the woman disappeared in a puff of sulfuric smoke.

Sofia Koen awakened from her deep slumber in the intensive care unit of Mercy Medical Center. She was dazed and confused. The last thing she remembered was being in her backyard speaking with Mavet while the children played. Her head was pounding and she was having difficulty breathing. She turned her head to see a nurse coming into the room.

"What am I doing here?" Sofia asked.

"You are very sick," the nurse replied.

"It is obvious that I am sick," Sofia coughed. "What is the matter with me?"

"I will locate a doctor…" the nurse started.

"I am asking you!" Sofia raised her voice.

"Calm down, ma'am. It is not good for you to get excited," the nurse put her hand on Sofia's arm in an attempt to settle her down.

"Where is my husband?"

"Ma'am, you were brought in as a Jane Doe. We did not know who to contact."

"My name is Sofia Koen. My husband is Levi Koen, the Superintendent of the Galena School System. Get him on the phone, now!"

"Yes, ma'am."

Sofia gave her Levi's cell phone number and watched her scurry out of the room and head toward the nurse's station to make the call. Her head was splitting and she closed her eyes. She wondered how long she had been in the hospital, away from her family. Who was taking care of them? How were they surviving without her at the helm of the tightly run ship? The house must be in shambles and the kids … She did not want to think about what could be going on in her home. She put her hand to her head; she wanted it to stop hurting. She fell asleep.

Sofia did not know how long she had been sleeping. When she opened her eyes, she saw Levi sitting in the chair close to her bed. He was holding her hand. It looked as if he had been crying when he looked up to see that she had awakened.

"Sofia, I did not know what was going on," he started.

"The last thing I remember is watching the kids playing in the yard," Sofia whispered.

Levi began to tell her what he knew of the afternoon of her disappearance. He told her that he drove up into the driveway and noticed that the winds had picked up, in the neighborhood. He looked toward the back of the house and noticed there was a great deal of debris flying around. He wondered where the debris was coming from, as he shut the car door and headed into the house. When he opened the door, the children were running in from the back patio. He assumed they were coming to greet him, so he took the time to acknowledge them. That was when he noticed the debacle in the back of the house.

He continued to tell her that he ushered the kids upstairs and headed out to see what was going on, just beyond the patio. He saw her in the throes of an intense argument with what appeared to be an apparition. He could not quite make out whether it was male or female. The person grabbed Sofia up by the neck and flung her into the wind and she disappeared into thin air. Levi stated that he ran out into the yard in pursuit of the offender, but he too vanished. After he left, the winds died down and things returned to normal.

He quickly returned to the house and dialed 911 to have someone come out to the house. They questioned him, extensively, as if he was a suspect in his wife's disappearance. He could not believe his ears, especially after the fantastic story he had relayed to the officers. The children were distraught when their mother did not return home for several weeks.

"They must be terrified," Sofia's voice sounded breathy.

"Well, they are children and they adapt very well. I have been getting a bunch of help from the members of the Wisdom Outreach Center.

God has kept us all well, while we waited for word from you; or about you."

"God has kept..." Sofia was gasping for breath. "When dir murni womta?"

"What are you saying, Sofia?" Levi looked concerned. He jumped up, ran to the door and called to the nurse.

"She is incoherent!" Levi yelled as the nurse rushed into the room.

Sofia's face drooped on one side and her eyes stared blankly toward the wall. The nurse checked her vitals and pushed the button on the side of the bed. A recorded voice spoke over the loud speaker, "CODE BLUE!" The machines on the side of her bed showed erratic readings before all of the data went flat.

"Sir, I am going to have to ask you to leave the room," the nurse escorted Levi into the hall as the medical staff rushed in with the crash cart. She closed the curtain behind her.

"Clear!"

Several moments passed, as the doctors and nurses worked to revive Sofia. Levi heard one of them say she had thrown a clot, which has caused his wife to have a stroke. He heard the machines restart and a steady heartbeat sounded, once more. A doctor opened the curtain and joined him in the hall.

"Mr. Koen, your wife came into the hospital suffering from infective endocarditis which is a very deadly form of a heart infection. We have been pushing high doses of antibiotics, in an attempt to quell the devastating effects of the infection. They have not been doing the job. She was in a coma, until today. It seems that she has suffered a stroke, which is a complication from the infection. Patients can develop embolisms that can break off and travel quickly to the brain or the lungs. In your wife's case, it went to her brain and has caused a massive stroke."

"She is too young to have a stroke," Levi said, to no one in particular.

"As I stated it was due to the infection in her heart. I do not want to give you false hope, Mr. Koen. Your wife may not survive through the night. The damage done to her heart valves, due to the infection and now the damage to her brain is quite extensive. You may want to gather the family together."

"Gather the family?"

"Yes, sir, to say their final goodbyes."

"How do you gather small children together to tell them that their mother is dying?"

"Is there someone we can call for you?"

Levi stumbled back to the wall behind him. He could not believe what he heard. How could his vibrant wife be dying? What was he supposed to tell his kids? He buried his face in his hands and cried. He did not want to believe what was happening in this moment. They were supposed to live out their dream, together. She had planned their life out to the letter and now she was not going to be around to see the fruit of her sacrifice. His cries echoed in the halls as he sunk to the floor. The doctor stood there with him, until he regained his composure.

"Is there anyone we can call for you, Mr. Koen?" The doctor asked, again.

"I will make the call myself, thank you doctor."

Levi walked toward the seating area of the intensive care unit. He decided he would call Pastor Zeke and his wife to pray for his wife. He was not going to tell the kids. Sofia had been gone for so long and they were beginning to adjust to life without her. He knew they would still awaken, in the night, calling for their mother. He would do what he had been doing since that dreadful afternoon. He would continue to tell them that their mommy loved them very much and if she could be with them, she would. He understood that as time went on that he would have to explain to them that their mother had been very sick and died, but right now, they were too young to process all of this.

The machines began screeching, again, in Sofia's room. Levi knew what was going on; his wife was dying and there was nothing to do about it.

"Time of death, nine thirty-seven," the doctor called.

CHAPTER TWENTY-FOUR

The day of Sofia Koen's funeral was dark and dreary. The clouds swirled as the forecasted thunderstorm made its way into Galena. Levi had asked one of the neighborhood teenagers to watch the children because he did not want them in attendance. He endured criticism for not informing the kids about their mother's death. He ignored people's judgments and did what he thought was best for his young family. He could not wrap his mind around her death, and he was a grown man. He did not want Hannah, Ahavah and Asher to see their mother in a casket or have to explain to them why she was descending in the ground.

One of the deacons of the Wisdom Outreach Center escorted Levi to the front of the sanctuary. He walked past Cale and Babette Richmond who sat quietly talking to the Palmers. Miles Kirkpatrick, Jarhys Houston, Gray Jenkins, Winter Pharron and Etmus Sadiyo sat in the row across from Sofia's extended family members. They were all lost in their own emotions, spawned by their own loss and bereavement. There had been too many funerals over the last several weeks - the last being for young Axel Fitzhugh. It was difficult to attend and watch his mother sit stoically in the front pew. She had to be lead in and out by the mayor of Galena, who could hardly contain his grief at the premature death of his son.

Pastor Zeke spoke of the spiritual attack that undertook the church and how desperately the congregants needed to inspect their lives. Death and destruction had found an opening and it was imperative to close the gap. They had been in prayer all week long because WOC was looking for a revival. They had started out on the right path and quickly lost their way. The word of the Lord, a few Sundays ago, made it plain that they had experienced a spiritual death that had made itself manifest in the natural; Analise Mitchell, Axel Fitzhugh, Maren Adley, Maddock Hamilton and Sofia Koen. The lives of those left behind would never be the same; and the pastor hoped and prayed that each person would draw closer to the Lord for comfort.

Ziva Montgomery stood with her husband at the front of the church. She wore a beautiful black and white summer suit with matching hat and shoes. Pastor Zeke had on a black suit with a crisp white shirt and a black, red and white tie. They made a striking couple as they waited for the procession to end. Zeke took Ziva's hand into his own and squeezed it, softly. He knew he was living on grace and nothing else. The enemy's plan was to take him out, in his sin, and leave his family in the gall of bitterness.

The First Lady quietly said a prayer of thanks, because she could have been in the seat of Levi Koen if God had not seen fit to raise her husband from his deathbed. Her heart went out to the widower and his children. She knew there was nothing that could prepare someone for the loss of his or her loved one, especially so young. The weeks prior to Levi knowing what happened to Sofia, he tormented himself thinking the worse. The reality of knowing is far more grueling than thought of it. With the thoughts, there was always the hint of hope that shone through the darkness of "what if." However, when the evidence slaps you in the face, it sucks the breath right out of your body. That is what she saw, this morning, a man desperate for a life sustaining breath. She moved closer to her husband and squeezed his hand, in return.

"There are no words that can reduce the fire of grief that runs amok in the heart of a man who has lost his wife. Only God knows what can be done to douse the inferno and cool the fevered brow," Pastor Zeke spoke. "We need to call on the name of the Lord for Levi; not just today but in the days and weeks to come."

Soft cries echoed throughout the church. Levi held himself and rocked, as his father patted him on the leg. His anguish was palpable. No one was untouched by the pain of his loss, as everyone sat in the church. Sobs escaped his lips as Pastor Zeke spoke of the emptiness that only God can fill.

Thunder began to rumble and lightening flashed outside of the building. The rains began to fall in sheets that ran down the windows. The skies had grown darker as the storm rolled in. The winds picked up and the sound of a metal garbage can tossed about boomed in the hallowed halls. A lone woman cried in the back of the church. A second, more robust, clap of thunder sounded, startling those in attendance.

The doors swung open, in the back of the church, and everyone turned to see whom the latecomer was that entered through the doors. It was Galia Fitzhugh, followed closely by her husband, Phineas. He whispered his apologies as she stormed to the front of the church. Her clothes were soaking wet and her hair clung to her face as a small river of black eye makeup ran down her cheeks. She did not have on any shoes and her pantyhose had long runs that traversed from foot to thigh.

"My son is dead," her voice slurred.

She walked over to Levi and knelt down in front of him.

"My son is dead, just like your wife is dead," the smell of alcohol wafted through the air.

Ziva walked over Galia and tried to help her up.

"Get your hands off of me!" Galia shouted. "You don't know what we are going through. Your husband is alive. Your children are alive."

"Galia, sweetie, come with me," Ziva persisted.

"You do not get to tell me what to do!" Galia stood up and swung her arm around pushing Ziva, causing her to stumble. "I am tired of you and your holier than thou attitude."

Ziva did not get offended. She knew the grief was talking for Galia. She would not allow herself to imagine life without her children. Axel Fitzhugh's funeral was one of the most difficult funerals she had to attend. His death greatly affected her daughter, as were many of the young people of the Wisdom Outreach Center. Marissa awakened, last night, by a nightmare that her brother had died instead of Axel. It was tough and all of the parents had to deal with the effects of his death, in their home.

"Galia," she said, softly.

In that moment, Galia Fitzhugh's body flung aside and the spirit of destruction stood in her stead. Mavet rose to his fullest stature, standing over Ziva Montgomery. She stepped back and Pastor Zeke pushed her behind him. At the furthest point of the church, another ominous figure erected from a seated position and headed toward the front of the sanctuary. He was moving quickly without feet touching the floor.

"Zeke, old buddy, you don't want to do this," Mavet snarled. "This has nothing to do with you; it is your wife that we have come for."

"We?" Zeke questioned.

Kaveid came to rest in front of the pastor and his wife. He looked from one to the other, trying to see where he could gain access.

Ziva had begun praying in the spirit when she realized that the spirit of destruction and the spirit of stubbornness had come into the church. These formidable imps required a strong foundation to withstand. She prayed that she had what it took to quench the fiery darts thrown by the demonic duo. She could feel the pressure in her mind to give in to fear and anxiety. She repeated the name of Jesus to herself.

"You have no place, in the house of God," Zeke commanded.

The two of them laughed and the building shook. They looked at one another then looked out into the congregation.

"We have many avenues into this place, Zeke," Mavet hissed. "There are a number of doors that allow us free reign to walk these aisles."

"You were one of those outlets, not that long ago," Kaveid joined in. "Mavet walked in, many times, with you and your family. You had an intimate relationship with him and you told him your deepest desires."

Ziva was listening and her resolve began to falter. How could Zeke allow such a thing to happen? Why would he entertain the enemy in such a manner and endanger the flock he commissioned to protect? How could she have been so blind as to not see the enemy at work in her own home?

"Yeah, not so sure now, are you Ziva?" Kaveid asked.

"Here you were thinking that you and your man were a fortified city; when in fact you were greatly divided," Mavet added.

"Don't listen to them, Ziva," Zeke was speaking. "Do not allow them to come in and cause division when God has restored us."

"Can you believe him, now? How can you know that he wasn't the one who invited us into the building?" Mavet was whispering in her ear. His hands were wrapping around her waist.

"You can't believe him, Ziva. He is untrustworthy. Everything you thought the two of you were building, he was tearing down with his own greed," Kaveid whispered in her other ear. His breath was so close that she could feel it travel down her canal.

"Ziva, God has delivered me. I have repented and asked for forgiveness," Zeke pleaded with his wife. "I have asked for your forgiveness and you granted it to me."

"Yes, I have, Zeke," Ziva said, softly.

Mavet stepped back, for a moment, as did Kaveid. He could see why his comrade had such a hard time with the woman. Her defenses were strong. She allowed God to govern her life in a way that very few did. Yet, they believed they were breaking away at the armor she wore. There had to be some chinks in it and they would find it.

"Think about the danger he put you and your children in, Ziva. I have been in your home. I was in your bedroom and sat down at your dinner table. He kept me hidden, from your prying eyes," Mavet moved in, once more. "While you were praying, he and I were conversing about plans for the Wisdom Outreach Center," he laughed. "You thought he only did that with you, didn't you?"

Kaveid could feel her soften under his hand, as it rested on her shoulder. He brushed her hair aside. He sniffed her scent and grimaced. He breathed in the fragrance of God, into his nostrils.

"There is therefore now no condemnation to them which are in Christ Jesus, who walk not after the flesh, but after the Spirit," Ziva spoke aloud. "It is not for me to hold on to and judge Zeke for the mistakes he made. God is our righteous judge."

Zeke turned to look his wife in the eyes. He implored her from the depths of his soul to lean on God and not heed the words of the demons that pressed her on every side. Her eyes locked onto his and he was concerned. He saw her struggle to believe in him after hearing such railing accusations. They bombarded her mind with thoughts and images meant to plant seeds of mistrust and betrayal. She begged him to speak to her spirit. She needed to believe in him and she was finding it difficult to hold on to her decision to forgive him.

"I love you and I know you love me, Ziva. God joined us together…"

"…and what God has joined together, let no man or demon, put asunder," Ziva felt her strength returning.

Zeke smiled and he prayed. He knew his wife was in serious warfare. He knew the enemy was convinced that if they could get her off her post that they would have the upper hand. She was the one that fought for the ministry and his life. She was the one who stood in the gap when he was preoccupied with his own desires. It was her faith and love for God that had brought him back from the brink of death. He needed her to hold on to God's hand as the enemy fought for her mind.

"Where was God, Ziva, when you were praying for your family and your husband was tearing down the walls of your defense?" Mavet was whittling his way between Ziva and Zeke.

"Why hold on to the love you once shared when he was so willing to throw it away for the church," Kaveid took both his hands and wrapped them around her waist. "Does he really love you the way Christ loves the church, Ziva," his whispers moved through her hair.

"My wife is dead," it started out a soft whispering voice. "My wife is dead," Levi's cries grew more intense. "MY WIFE IS DEAD!!!" He jumped up from the front row and ran toward Sofia's casket.

"My son is dead!" Galia yelled out.

"My Analise is gone!" Miles bellowed from the back.

"Maren is dead and where is God?" Adley questioned with the pain evident in his words.

The attendants of the funeral moaned and groaned. They wailed and cried. They tore at their clothes and their hair. Grief and anguish was running up and down the aisles touching everyone in their reach. Chaos bounced off the walls and ricocheted off the tormented souls. Ziva could not focus. She felt like she was suffocating. She felt closed in on all sides.

She reached for Zeke and he reached out, in return, but could not pull her to himself. Cale Richmond ran full speed to the front of the church and ripped at Ziva's clothes. His eyes were wild and he did not seem in control of his faculties. Her hat hurled to the floor, as the circuit court judged mauled at her.

"Let me have her!" He yelled out.

It was the moment needed. Ziva knocked off center and could not focus on what was happening. Mavet and Kaveid seized the opportunity and grabbed the First Lady up in their clutches. They soared above the dissonance that was taking place, as their comrades had come to their aid. She could not wrench free of their grasp, as she hung in the air between stubborn destruction. Kaveid held her mouth while Mavet kept his hands on her head. They needed to block out any attempt to call on the name of her God.

They were heading toward the door with who they thought was their only obstacle between them and the whole town of Galena, when Marissa Montgomery burst through the door.

She stood between the demons and their way of escape with a look of determination on her face.

"NOT ON MY WATCH!" She yelled out in complete authority.

EPILOGUE

"O Lord, my God – the God of Abraham, Isaac and Jacob – the God of Israel. You are enthroned in the heavens and sit as Sovereign Ruler of all the kingdoms of the earth. Incline Your ear to hear and open Your eyes to see what and who seeks to come against Your children. We are the sheep of Your pasture – You are our Shepherd – Our Strong Defender – We are safe. Nothing by any means shall harm us – No weapon that has been formed, is being formed, or plans to be formed in the future shall prosper. We are forever under Your watchful eye. You know who has set their strength against us, and who purposes to be of no good to us – thwart the plans of the enemy, right now in the name of Jesus. Send out Your angels and scatter them a thousand ways, until they surrender under the mighty hand of Your army. We will not seek to intrude on Your territory. We will not seek to introduce our ideas and thoughts into Your perfect plan. We will not seek to save ourselves – You have already done that, on Calvary. We are redeemed. We are empowered. We are holy and righteous, not by any deeds of our own, but by the blood of Jesus. We are blood washed and blood bought, ransomed from a sinner's grave by Your love. Forgive us for going against Your plans, every time we sought to figure You out. Forgive us for choosing our way when we did not understand Yours. Forgive us for allowing religion and selfish desire to govern us when You sought relationship. Forgive us when we allowed our manners and customs to dictate how we heard and responded to You. Forgive us for conforming to this world and its systems when You wanted us to live higher. Forgive us for complaining. Forgive us for giving up the search for You when You remained silent to our flesh. Forgive us for lying when we said we trusted You all the while making our own plans when You told us to be still. We come to You with fresh eyes and a yielded spirit. We want to see what You show us and allow our spirit to be in tune with Your Holy Spirit. We refuse to be led by our flesh and what we detect with our natural senses. We submit to You training us to be lead by Your eye, ever diligent to be looking to You and not our circumstances and those around us. We will not seek the approval of those around us, when we have clearly heard Your instructions. We are sons and daughters, not mere children. Thank You for Your ever present patience and long-suffering. Thank You for Your grace and mercy. Thank You for Your goodness toward us. We receive Your favor and defer our will to Yours. In Jesus' name – AMEN"